Twisted

Logan Hall

For Alexis,
my greatest supporter and the heart behind every word.

1

The phone slipped from Ava's hand like an after thought, her ragged breath the only sound in the room. Whether it was with prospective families or open cases, she needed a moment to ground herself after each call. As a receptionist for the Children's Rescue Alliance, a growing organization dedicated to assisting families with missing children and advocating for child welfare policies, she found the emotional weight of the job demanding.

This time of year was always particularly hard, especially as the anniversary of that day approached. Memories fought their way to the surface as her stomach churned. Forcing them down was a necessity, especially while at work. The sudden jangle of the phone snapped her back to the present. Her voice slid into its usually honeyed smoothness, masking the turmoil beneath.

"Hello, my name is Ava and thank you for calling the Children's Rescue Alliance. How can I help you today?"

A deep, husky voice on the other end answered, "Hello, Ava. I don't know how often you are told this, but you have the most beautiful voice I've ever heard."

It took only a second for Ava to identify the speaker, letting his silky words caress her soul and ignite a flame in her core that only he could satisfy. She did a quick survey of the spacious lobby to make sure that no clients were in one of the plush, black leather sofas or armchairs. After her sweep revealed that no one was around, she returned her attention to the man on the phone.

Ava bit her lip, and said coyly, "Well, thank you for the compliment. I have been told that my voice is angelic."

The man's amused huff made her cheeks flush with warmth and sent a shiver down her slender arms. "As much as I love playing this game with you Ava, we do have a dinner reservation in a couple of hours and I wanted to make sure that we are still on for tonight."

Ava chuckled, "Of course, Carter, I'll be getting off work soon and then I'll head to our meeting spot." She slid a strand of her straight, shoulder-length brown hair behind her ear.

Carter hesitated before finally asking, "How have you been doing today? I know this week has always been pretty hard on you."

"I've been okay. I've just been trying to focus on work and getting through the day. How's work been for you?"

She could hear jack hammers, bulldozers, and other construction noise in the background. "It's been good! We've been making some solid progress on this fancy theater the city has been trying to get built for the past couple of years."

Ava smiled, "Please be safe. I don't want my boyfriend to be crushed by steel beams or whatever it is you use to build stuff."

Carter laughed, "I always am. I'm about to finish up for the day, so I'm heading home to shower. I don't think showing up covered in dirt, wearing overalls and a hard hat, would be too appropriate for where we're going."

She tried not to laugh at the image that played in her mind and said, "Alright, I'll see you soon. I love you, Carter."

"See you soon and I love you, too."

After Carter hung up, Ava glanced at the clock on the wall to her right: 4:30 p.m. She surveyed the waiting room, divided by the walkway from the door to her desk. Magazines were scattered across the couches on both sides, the trash can near the door was full, and the TV in the section to her right was tuned to a newscast. As she tidied up the waiting areas, she occasionally listened to the news playing on the television.

"In other news, there has been another gruesome discovery of mutilated bodies......no apparent connections between the victims and all are missing items from their bodies......the authorities have no leads or suspects as of this taping and are urging citizens to be cautious......"

Ava switched off the television and glanced at the clock: 5:00 pm. She walked towards the entrance, and when she reached the smooth oak door, she swept her gaze around the waiting room areas to confirm everything was clean and tidy. With an approving nod, she turned the golden doorknob and stepped into the embrace of a sun-kissed Autumn day.

Ava closed her eyes and took a moment to soak up the warmth of the sun and the gentle breeze. She opened her eyes, feeling lighter, and made her way to the bus stop in front of her workplace. The trees lining the street provided a beautiful backdrop as she waited, their green leaves slowly changing color. She always loved autumn more than the other seasons; she enjoyed gazing at the rich oranges, deep reds, and dazzling yellows before the leaves fell from the trees.

Ava heard the rumble of the bus up the street and turned her attention from the foliage. After it hissed to a stop, the door slid open and Ava climbed aboard. She nodded to the bus driver, a portly older man, and dropped her fare into the black box next to his seat. She scanned the packed bus and sighed with relief when she spotted a row of empty seats. She didn't mind sitting with someone, but she always preferred riding alone after a long day of work.

For the first few minutes, Ava felt at ease as the bus rolled forward. The changing colors, serene ponds with ducks, all provided a sense of calmness out her window. That is until, inevitably, her mind drifted back to the nightmare that was the day everything shifted.

Ava tried to pull away from the memory that was resurfacing, but was powerless as the passing trees and ponds hypnotized her.

A blood-curdling scream in the distance jolted her awake from her nap. She sat up abruptly, recognizing that voice. Ava scanned the living room to see if Oliver was near, but she was alone. This isn't right. She doesn't even remember falling asleep.

Ava stood up from the couch and ran to the foyer. The giant, ornate double doors were wide open. She started having trouble breathing, her heartbeat unbearably loud in her ears. No, no, no this can't be happening. She started shouting, "Oli-"

The sudden jolt from the bus stopping pulled Ava out of her nightmare. Sweat beaded her forehead and her throat felt dry, as if she were screaming. Her nervous glance at the people filing out of the bus assured her that none were giving her a second thought. A quick look out the window identified this stop as the one in Mayfield, London. She quickly jumped out of her seat and headed towards the exit, the foul memory receding with every step. After she stepped off, she surveyed her surroundings to figure out the direction she needed to go, but her eyes snagged on a man that was sitting on a bench to the left of her bus.

When she recognized the black sweep of hair and chiseled facial features that resembled a Greek gods' statue, a big grin started spreading across her face. The man stood up, a smile answering her own, as she started running towards him. Ava flung herself into him, breathing in his earthy scent of cedarwood and musk as he spun her around.

She pulled back and kissed him deeply, fully aware of the other people around them. As she withdrew, she let him see the burning hunger in her eyes. His mouth quirked to the side, as if he could read her thoughts and said, "Well, hello to you too, Ava."

Ava said, a little too innocently, "What can I say? I just missed you so much since the last time I saw you."

Carter, in mock disbelief, said, "You saw me two days ago."

Ava caressed her hand down his muscular chest and purred, "And that's two days too many. I want to see you every day."

He swept his gaze over her body, starting with her full breasts, slightly exposed by the low-cut of her dress. His eyes moved down her curves, accentuated by the skin-tight blue fabric, to her long, tan legs, which were left bare.

As if suddenly remembering they were in public, Carter brought his gaze up to hers, his emerald eyes sparkling with mischief as he laughed. "I want to see you every day, too! Maybe we can make that happen soon." He gave her a sly wink. "But we really should head to the restaurant if we want to make the reservation."

Ava disentangled herself from Carter and mockingly pouted, "Don't tease me like that." She turned on her heel and started down the cobblestone street toward the restaurant. She heard Carter chuckle softly to himself and soon felt him catch up, falling into step beside her.

They walked in companionable silence as Ava slipped her arm through his. The street was softly illuminated by twinkling lights strung between ornate lamp posts, casting warm, flickering shadows on the elegant townhouses that lined the cobblestone street. The townhouses, with their ivy-clad facades and detailed brickwork, looked even more charming against the backdrop of the dimming sky. An early fall breeze, crisp with the hint of approaching winter, rustled the leaves scattered on the ground and carried the subtle scent of damp earth and mist. Ava's gaze wandered over the other couples strolling hand-in-hand, their soft laughter blending with the gentle murmur of the evening and the distant sounds of London settling into its night rhythm.

After about ten minutes, they arrived at their destination: a bustling restaurant with a line extending out the door. Ava caught glimpses of white tables set with fine china, stylishly dressed patrons, and the soft glow of flickering candles that created a warm, inviting atmosphere inside.

This was the best in the city and always required a reservation weeks in advance.

Ava looked up to Carter, a smile on her face, and said coyly, "Remind me, why are we here again? What special occasion are we celebrating that requires five star dining?"

Carter tipped his head down toward her, a half-smile on his full lips. "Well, we have been dating for the past year and a half. I figure that is something worth celebrating, don't you?"

Nostalgia overtook Ava as she replied, "It sure is. You have no idea how happy this past year has made me."

Carter leaned to kiss her cheek and whispered, "I love you, too." When they reached the entrance of the restaurant, Ava stopped abruptly, a sickening feeling of being watched creeping over her.

She turned around to face the street and murmured to Carter, "You go ahead without me, I'll catch up in a minute."

Her ears seemed to hollow out as a roaring noise flooded her mind, muffling the sounds of the bustling street around her. She saw a young man across the street, staring at her with a large, unsettling smile. Carter murmured something that sounded like concern but began to turn away.

Quickly, Ava reached behind her, grasping his arm, her voice trembling with fear as she whispered, "Wait, don't go."

2

Carter was instantly at her side, his voice laced with concern. "What is it? Is everything okay?"

Ava felt like she couldn't breathe, that a giant boulder was crushing her chest. She studied the young man—his long, curly brown hair, short, round nose, almond-shaped eyes, and angular face. She couldn't believe it. It was him, older, a glimpse of who he might have become.

Ava said breathlessly, "Do you see him? That man across the street, staring at me." She was shaking as Carter scanned the street.

He murmured, "I'm sorry, honey, but I don't see anyone." Ava was about to object when a bus passed, obscuring the man. When it moved on, he had disappeared. She realized she had been holding her breath and sagged with relief as the feeling of being watched vanished. It must have been her mind playing tricks.

Ava had been under a lot of stress recently, as she always has been for the past six years. The week leading up to the anniversary of the incident always made her feel like she was carrying a weight on her shoulders and caused her stomach to be in a constant state of upheaval.

Carter pulled her to his side and guided her into the restaurant. She distantly registered his voice soothing her and leaned her head against his broad, muscled shoulder. By the time they sat down at their table, she was feeling more like herself.

After delectable dishes of roasted lamb, vegetables, and herb-seasoned mashed potatoes, Ava felt as though she might explode. She thought she wouldn't be able to eat another bite until Carter ordered a German chocolate cake to share, and her stomach promptly made room for dessert. As they waited for it to arrive, they talked about everything and nothing—reminiscing about old memories, sharing their thoughts on recent events, and laughing over lighthearted stories. Their conversation flowed easily, filled with warmth and affection, and soon they fell into a comfortable silence, simply enjoying each other's presence.

Ava tucked a strand of her hair behind her ear and said, "I'm sorry if I made you worry earlier. I thought I saw someone I used to know."

Carter's round eyes softened as he said gently, "It's okay. I'm just glad that you are feeling better." His brows scrunched together, as if internally debating something, and asked cautiously, "Can I ask who you thought you saw?"

Ava had never shared the full extent of what happened almost seven years ago with anyone, except for Carter. When they first met, she had confided in him about the basics, but even he only knew the surface details.

He was unaware of the deep torment she carried inside. Just thinking about it almost consumed her with guilt and sorrow, feelings so overwhelming they threatened to destroy her. Yet, as she looked at Carter's handsome face, the man she loved, she decided that she could face that darkness within herself to let him in.

Ava took a shuddering breath and, steeling herself, said, "As you know, almost seven years ago, I was an au pair for a thirteen year old boy, Oliver. I was only twenty-one at the time and I loved him. I saw him as my younger brother, my family." Her voice broke, and she felt something in herself start to crack. Carter extended a hand over the table, a silent invitation. Ava grabbed his hand and he became an anchor in the storm brewing in her heart.

Ava continued, "You would have liked him. He was such a sweet boy who loved to play games and be outside. We would watch movies together and build Lego sets. It was the best year of my life. One day, I fell asleep in the living room—I didn't even mean to. At that point, I had been with them for a year and I had never fallen asleep before. I woke up to Oliver screaming from outside, but I was too groggy to get up."

Tears started streaming down her face as she struggled to keep her emotions under control. She wanted to break down and rant at the unfairness of the world. Before she could lose control, Carter placed his other hand over hers and comforted her, saying, "Hey, I'm right here. I'm with you, and you're safe."

Ava took a long moment to compose herself, studying Carter as she did. She saw admiration and pride shining in his eyes. She whispered, "Thank you, Carter." Before she could say more, the waiter arrived with their dessert, but neither of them reached for the forks.

She dipped her head down and continued, "When I was finally able to get up, I ran outside and saw a patch of blood at the bottom of the stairs. I looked everywhere but couldn't find him. I knew in my bones that something was wrong. When his parents came home, I told them I couldn't find him. His dad searched the surrounding woods, and his mother fell to the ground in tears, blaming me for his disappearance. When his father returned, they called the police."

Ava's voice hitched as she held back tears. "The police couldn't find his body, even after weeks of searching the woods. I don't know if you remember, but when we first met, I mentioned that they officially declared him dead. His parents couldn't handle it and ended up taking their own lives—his mother overdosed on sleeping pills, and his father shot himself with his pistol."

Ava looked up at Carter with tear-stained cheeks and croaked, "I may have just been his au pair, but Oliver became my family. I failed him that day. I fell asleep and couldn't protect him. Sometimes it's all too much, and I feel like I can't continue living with all this guilt. It feels like life isn't worth living."

She stilled as Carter tenderly brought her slender hand to his lips and kissed it softly. His thumb caressed her fingers, and his green eyes seemed to pierce right into her soul. He said firmly, yet gently, "You are the bravest person I've ever met. What happened wasn't your fault. It was a tragedy, but not your fault. Thank you for telling me." His smooth voice wrapped around her like an invisible hug. "I know it was hard, and I appreciate your willingness to share. I love you, Ava."

Ava used her free hand, which had stopped quivering, to wipe her mascara-stained face. "I love you too, Carter. You are worth facing the bad memories." Ava turned her attention to the German chocolate cake, a decadent slice layered with rich, fudgy chocolate and topped with a glossy coconut-pecan frosting that glistened under the dim restaurant light.

Quickly picking up the closest fork, she said through a wicked smile, "Since I shared so much with you, I think I should get all the cake."

Carter's mouth matched hers and picked up the other fork. "Oh, I don't think so." They laughed as they playfully fought for the chocolate cake, their forks flashing in the warm overhead lights. The bad memories quickly faded away as Ava focused on this moment with Carter, the person with whom she felt safest.

After he paid the bill, they left the restaurant hand-in-hand. She leaned into his arm, savoring the warmth that radiated from him. As they chatted on the way back to her home, Ava reflected on the dinner with Carter. She hadn't expected to share the depths of her despair and guilt, but she was glad she did. Ava felt as though their relationship had taken a step forward, overcoming an obstacle she hadn't realized was in their path.

Before she realized it, having been lost in thought and conversation, they arrived at her home—an aged two-story townhouse. The building featured a classic brick façade with a charming wrought-iron railing along the narrow front steps. Two balconies, draped in ivory vines, were adorned with a few potted plants, adding a touch of greenery against the weathered brick. The large windows had wooden shutters painted a soft shade of blue, and the doorway was framed by an ornate, period-appropriate arch.

They stopped at the base of the stairs; Ava was lost in his gaze. Gently tucking a stray strand of hair behind her ear, he said, "There's something I wanted to ask you."

Ava raised a thin eyebrow as she caught his hand and teased, "Oh? And what might that be?"

He interlaced their hands and smiled. "You are the most important person in my life. I couldn't imagine living without you. You make me incredibly happy, and I want to spend the rest of my life with you." Ava held her breath as he dropped to one knee and pulled out a black velvet box. As he opened the box, the soft glow of a single, exquisite diamond ring was revealed.

The ring featured a brilliant round-cut diamond set in a delicate band of white gold, with tiny pave diamonds encrusting the band. The stone itself seemed to capture and refract the light, casting a mesmerizing array of colors. Ava felt like her chest was going to explode as she gazed at the radiant gem. "Ava Collins, will you make me the luckiest man in the world and marry me?"

Her knees threatened to give out as emotion surged through her. Tears streamed down her face as she breathed, "Yes, I will."

Carter grinned and quickly stood to slide the ring onto her delicate finger. Ava couldn't tear her gaze away from the dazzling diamond, its brilliance reflecting the promise of their future together. The thought that she was going to spend the rest of her life with him filled her with overwhelming joy.

He gently tipped her chin and pressed a soft, lingering kiss to her lips. With passion burning in his eyes, Carter whispered, "I love you, Ava."

"I love you too, Carter." Her smile took on a mischievous glint as she added, "How about we celebrate by popping open the bottle of champagne I've been saving for a special occasion?"

＊＊＊＊＊＊＊＊＊＊＊＊＊＊

Later that night, Ava and Carter were in the kitchen, their laughter and chatter mingling with the soft clinking of glasses. They were finally getting around to opening the champagne, a celebratory bottle that had been waiting for a special occasion.

As Ava poured the wine, the cozy warmth of the kitchen was abruptly interrupted by a loud thunk outside the front door. She stopped pouring, her hand resting on Carter's as she froze.

Her eyes whipped to the door, and she whispered, "Did you hear that?"

Carter muttered, "Yeah, I did. Let me go check it out." Ava stayed silent as he crept toward the door, silently easing it open. He turned back to her and said, "It's all clear out here, but come check this out."

Ava stepped out onto the porch and drew in a sharp breath. A large, weathered hunting knife with a rugged, wooden handle had been driven into the door frame, its blade glinting ominously in the light. An envelope was pinned beneath it. With trembling hands, she yanked the knife out, the blade making a metallic scrape as it slid free, and caught the letter as it fluttered to the ground.

She ripped open the envelope and quickly scanned the contents. Her breath caught in her throat as she nearly dropped it, her hands shaking uncontrollably. Inside, Polaroids of her and Carter and a document made from cut out letters from magazines were marred with blood.

The threat made her blood run cold.

Tell Carter or the police about the letter and he would be killed. The writer had included his address as proof. Alongside the threat, the letter contained an invitation to a dinner party, detailing the date, time, dress code, and location.

Before Carter could catch a glimpse of the invitation, she quickly folded it in half. The worry etched across his face was unmistakable as he studied her. "Is everything okay? What did the envelope say?"

Ava, hating every word that came out of her mouth, lied, "Oh, it's nothing. Just an invitation to a murder mystery dinner party that one of my friends is hosting. They must have used the knife for dramatic effect. "

3

A few days later, Ava sat across from her friends Ashley and Samantha in a bustling bistro. The place was alive with the hum of conversation and the clink of silverware, its checkered black-and-white tiles and cozy red leather booths adding to its charm. Vintage jazz played softly in the background, mingling with the rich aroma of freshly brewed coffee and pastries.

As she recounted the unsettling story of finding a knife driven into her door frame, Ashley, her long strawberry-blonde hair falling over her face, pushed it back from her wide, blue eyes, which were now full of shock. Her freckled cheeks turned pale as she absorbed the disturbing details. Samantha, with her round eyes and dark, arched brows, stared at Ava in disbelief, her face frozen in a mix of surprise and concern.

After a few moments of tense silence, Ashley said, "Wow, I'm sorry that happened to you. At least Carter was there."

Samantha nodded in agreement, her brown curls bouncing with the movement. "What are you going to do about it? Are you going to the police?"

Ava rubbed her neck and said, "I don't know. I told him it was just an invitation to a dinner party from one of my friends, but I don't feel right lying to him." She leaned her head in her hand, a look of frustration crossing her face. "Do you think there's any chance it could have been a prank by Damian or Lucas?"

Ashley tilted her head to the side. "I doubt it. While it sounds like something they'd do, I don't think they would have gone so far as to stalk you and take those photos."

Samantha pushed her square glasses up her nose and gently asked, "Could it be related to Oliver's death? The anniversary is coming up soon." Ava stared at her closest friends.

After the Wellingtons kicked her out of their house, Ava moved to London to start over. She eventually became friends with Ashley and Samantha, who introduced her to Damian and Lucas. Damian, with his tousled dark hair and easy charm, quickly became someone she could rely on. Lucas, more reserved with his sharp, attentive eyes and thoughtful demeanor, offered a steady presence during a turbulent time.

Over time, they became like family to her. Once she felt comfortable, she opened up about the day Oliver disappeared. When the news broke almost two years ago that Oliver was presumed dead, Damian and Lucas, along with Ashley and Samantha, were there to support her, helping her piece together the fragments of her soul.

Ava rubbed her temples and took a slow sip of her steaming coffee, the rich aroma of freshly ground beans filling her senses. The warmth of the mug seeped into her fingers as she breathed in the comforting scent. "I don't know. It's possible, but I don't know who would be out to get me. Before they died, I hadn't spoken to Oliver's parents or his family." She let out a frustrated sigh. "I don't know what to do. Should I go? Should I not go? If I tell Carter, he's dead. If I tell the police, he's dead. If I don't go, then I assume he'd be dead. I mean, the best case is that it's a prank by Damian, right? I just hate lying to him. It's been eating me alive."

Ashley reached over, her long strawberry-blonde hair falling across her face as she gently took Ava's hand. "I don't know, but we're here for you. If you decide not to go and tell the police, the four of us will make sure to protect Carter. No one would stand a chance against us."

Her gaze dropped to the sparkling ring on Ava's finger, and her expression shifted from worry to sheer excitement. She gasped and leaned in closer, her voice a mix of disbelief and delight. "Did he propose to you? When? How? You've got to tell us everything, girl!"

Samantha quickly set her coffee cup aside and reached out to grab Ava's hand. Her eyes sparkled with genuine excitement as she exclaimed, "It's beautiful!"

Ava's mind drifted from their conversation as she started recounting the proposal. Her eyes lit up, and a smile spread across her face as she relived the moment. Her heart swelled with joy, thinking about the life she would get to share with Carter. For a moment, everything else faded away, leaving only the warmth and excitement of their future together.

Samantha leaned back in the booth, adjusting her glasses as they slipped down her nose. Her dark hair, tied back in a neat ponytail, swayed slightly with her movement. She let out a dramatic groan. "Ugh, that's too sweet. Why can't I find a man like that?"

Ava laughed and teased, "It's because they're all intimidated by your intelligence. Although, I bet you'd have a shot with Damian."

Ashley slapped her hand on the table, her laughter ringing out as she shook her head. "Talk about a match made in heaven! You two would be so cute together."

Her eyes sparkled with amusement, and she leaned in, still chuckling at the thought.

Ava let her mind settle in the moment, savoring the laughter and camaraderie as they went back and forth. Although she was still uncertain about what to do regarding the invitation, she was determined not to let it overshadow the joy of being with her precious friends.

4

A week after receiving the invitation, Ava arrived at the designated location. The decision to attend alone had torn her apart, but she couldn't jeopardize Carter's safety. His well-being was her top priority.

All week, he had been probing for details about her plans—where she was going, which friend organized it, the timing, and more. Each time he questioned her, Ava forced a bright, convincing smile and delivered evasive answers, her heart aching with every lie.

As the taxi rumbled down the long, gravel driveway, Ava's gaze fixed on the looming structure ahead. Through the windows, she could see the building's shell, its grandeur faded over time. Her heart sank as she took in the dismal state of the grounds.

The gardens, once lush and vibrant, were now a tangled mess of weeds. The hedges, which had once been neatly trimmed, were wild and unkempt. The lawn, once a pristine expanse of emerald green, was now a patchwork of brown and overgrown with age, reflecting the neglect that had settled over the place.

As Ava's taxi glided into the circular entryway, her heart sank at the sight of the grand multi-tiered fountain. Once a centerpiece of splendor, it now stood dry and weathered, its elaborate details obscured by layers of grime. The sight triggered a surge of memories, vivid and unrelenting, replaying in her mind like a film she couldn't stop.

She and Oliver splashing and floating in the once-pristine waters of the fountain, their laughter echoing through the countryside's quiet. She remembered chasing him through the soft, verdant grass, their bare feet tickling the lush blades in a carefree game of tag. There were scenes of Oliver helping her harvest plump tomatoes, cucumbers, and other vegetables from the garden, their hands working together in a vibrant world that now felt like a distant dream.

She managed to regain control of her emotions, shoving those bittersweet memories deep within herself. Yet, as her gaze fell upon the manor before her, tears threatened to spill. The once-beautiful estate was now a shadow of its former self. The boarded-up windows and dirty facade stood in stark contrast to the pristine manor she remembered. The bushes that had once framed the foundation were now lifeless and withered. The paint on the columns, once white and pristine, was peeling away, revealing the weathered wood beneath. The brick walls were chipped and worn, encrusted with grime and dirt, their former splendor all but erased.

Ava snapped out of her daze when the taxi driver announced their arrival. After thanking and paying him, she stepped out of the vehicle, only to be overcome by a strange sensation. A tingling numbness spread through her body, and she began to hear ghostly whispers swirling around her. It felt as though a malevolent presence was hovering just beyond her consciousness.

She was paralyzed with fear, her breath caught in her throat. But just as abruptly as it had begun, the eerie sensation vanished, leaving her standing in uneasy silence.

Ava attributed the unsettling experience to her frayed nerves and the foreboding atmosphere. As she glanced around, her eyes fell on the line of luxury cars already parked, their sleek, polished exteriors a stark contrast to her humble taxi. A wave of shame washed over her, intensified by the realization that she had arrived in such an ordinary vehicle. This sense of inadequacy quickly blossomed into dread as she faced the daunting task of entering the manor and mingling with the affluent guests.

She glanced down at her floral sundress, the fabric soft but showing signs of wear, with its faded print and frayed hem. Her worn, nude heels, scuffed from years of use, only highlighted her sense of being out of place. The dress, with its modest neckline and delicate, pastel flowers, seemed starkly insufficient compared to what she imagined the other guests would be wearing.

Ava checked her watch: 4:30 p.m. There were still thirty minutes until the party started, but she wasn't ready to face everyone inside just yet. Her eyes fell on the area that held a quaint garden and pond to the left of the manor. She made her way toward the fenced-in area, the gravel crunching under her feet.

It struck Ava as odd that there were no birds singing and no whisper of the wind—just an eerie silence. As she reached the gate, she noticed the wood was rough and splintered, with the locking mechanism missing from the front. She pushed the rusted handle forward, the cold biting at her skin, and tried not to cringe at the shrieking of the metal hinges.

She stepped into the garden area, the smell of rot filling her nostrils, and made her way toward the still, cracked pond. She carefully sidestepped overturned, broken chaise lounge chairs that had once been used to relax and enjoy the fragrant basil, oregano, and other herbs growing in the garden. The only sound now was the faint rustle of dead leaves and the unsettling stillness that replaced the babbling stream.

Ava noticed that the pots housing the variety of herbs had been smashed on the ground, as if someone had thrown them at random in a fit of rage. At least, she assumed so from the apparent dents in the wooden fence and the chipped brick wall of the house.

She reached the pond and stared at her muted reflection. Her normal cheerful features looked dull against the backdrop of the lifeless pond. The pond was choked with dead algae, and the plants had all withered; the water was completely still, as if frozen in time. Ava could make out the outlines of the koi fish—now just bones—that used to mesmerize Oliver. She used to relish the sunny, warm days spent in this little haven, watching Oliver study the fish while she lounged comfortably on a chair.

She supposed that those days had long been replaced by the constant, oppressive gray sky that leeched color from her skin and surroundings. Everything seemed so muted to Ava. Lost in these thoughts, she didn't hear the footsteps approaching from behind.

A gruff voice suddenly cut through her reverie.

"Who the hell are you and what are you doing here?"

5

Ava turned around and froze. An imposing man with muscles straining against his black suit loomed over her. The jagged scar running from the edge of his close-cropped black hair to the bridge of his nose looked like a mad man's exclamation point.

Ava, still at a loss for words, guessed he was in his late twenties or early thirties. His gaze swept over her with the cold, calculating intensity of a predator sizing up its prey.

She regained her composure but couldn't suppress the stutter as she said, "I-I-I'm Ava Collins. I-I used to w-work here years a-ago." The man's eyes flashed with what seemed like surprise and recognition. Ava began to back up, but the man raised his broad hands, palms up, in a calming gesture.

His tawny eyes locked onto hers, pinning her in place. "I'm not going to hurt you. I apologize for startling you," he said. Ava saw no deceit in his gaze, and her racing heart began to calm, though she still eyed him warily.

The man extended a tanned hand and said softly, "My name is Luiz Garcia, and I'm a lawyer from Spain." Ava had noted the thick accent earlier but couldn't place it. She took his hand and gave it a quick shake.

They stared at each other in awkward silence until Ava, crossing her arms, asked shyly, "So, what is an attorney from Spain doing out in the English countryside?"

Luiz's thin eyebrows scrunched together. "I received a mysterious letter that invited me to this… event. I don't know who the host is, as the invitation didn't have a name on it."

Ava chuckled. "Why would you come all the way out here from Spain to attend a dinner party hosted by an unknown person?"

Luiz put a hand on his neck and laughed nervously. "I was planning on taking a vacation anyway, and the idea of the countryside seemed relaxing at the time. It looks like I should have chosen a different destination."

Ava wanted to ask if his invitation had a threatening note attached to it too, but she thought it best to keep it to herself in case he was the one threatening her. She couldn't help but feel uneasy about Luiz, as if he were hiding something.

Ava laughed weakly. "Indeed, this place seems dreadful." She paused for a moment, debating internally, and then asked, "By chance, do you know anything about who else will be here?"

Luiz pressed his mouth into a thin line and replied, "I have a few ideas about who might be here, but I can't say for certain."

Ava hummed to herself as the space began to feel suffocating. "Then maybe it's time to go introduce ourselves to our mystery host and the other guests." Feigning bravado, she stepped around Luiz's imposing figure and exited the forlorn garden.

She heard him pause for a moment, mutter something in Spanish, and then follow her. She rounded the corner of the house and climbed the grimy stone steps. Reaching the massive, dark mahogany double doors, she noticed that the once-flowing, intricate patterns had faded due to the elements.

Ava stared at the worn patterns and reached out with a tentative hand. As her fingers touched the door, it creaked open on a phantom wind. The groan of the doors made the house seem like a beast stirring to life, ready to devour her. The foyer's gloom drew her trembling body in as if by magnetic attraction.

As her eyes adjusted to the gloom, she gasped at the contrast that greeted her. Sophisticated sconces spaced evenly along the walls held flickering candles, casting a warm, dancing light and deep shadows across the room. The deep brown wood floor gleamed with polish, and not a single speck of dust marred its surface, nor was there any on the plush, cream-colored carpet that lay in the center of the room.

The furniture and sitting chairs were pristine; a large, ornate wooden settee with richly upholstered fabric stood elegantly along one wall, and high-backed armchairs with intricate carvings flanked a grand mahogany writing desk. It was as if nothing had changed in the past seven years, except for two glaring differences.

Ava looked up to find the once-bright crystal chandelier hanging in the center of the foyer now completely dark, its prisms casting no light. She then noticed the sculpted marble table, which was usually adorned with large bouquets of flowers, now held only a simple placard with a black arrow pointing to the left.

Ava felt a shiver of unease at the immaculate state of the manor's interior. Who had cleaned the house so thoroughly? Why the stark contrast between the neglected exterior and the pristine interior? Her skin crawled with the feeling of being watched, but the biggest question loomed in her mind: Who had invited her here, and why? Her mind whirling, she followed the direction of the arrow.

Approaching the archway leading to the living room, she heard a murmur of hushed voices emanating from within. Gathering her resolve, she stepped through the archway. The moment she entered, the voices fell silent. Ava took a deep breath and began to scan her surroundings, her gaze taking in every detail of the room.

The warmth from the blazing fire in the fireplace on the right wall chased away the chill Ava hadn't noticed since stepping inside. She quickly scanned the room, taking in the four people present.

A petite, beautiful young woman with wavy, golden hair sat in a plush, red armchair facing the fire. Her features were hidden in the shadows, but Ava guessed she was no older than twenty-three. The woman seemed lost in her own world, her blank stare fixed on the flames.

On the back wall, a balding, portly man with a pudgy face sat nervously in a simple armchair. His charcoal jacket, though well-tailored, looked worn. Sweat beaded on his bushy eyebrows and mustache as he dabbed at them with a white handkerchief, his eyes wide with apprehension.

Ava's gaze shifted to an older woman she recognized as the former maid of Oliver's family, now wearing a simple gray dress. The silver locket hanging from her slim neck caught the light, but her long, pointed nose and angular face made her look birdlike. The disdain in her eyes was unmistakable as she scrutinized Ava.

Finally, a young man she identified as the former gardener from the estate stood beside the maid. His lanky frame fidgeted in a brown corduroy suit, and his eyes were filled with guilt as he shook slightly, as though he had seen a ghost.

Luiz stepped around Ava and positioned himself at the corner of the fireplace nearest to the archway. He observed the room quietly, his only sign of surprise being a blink and the pressing of his lips into a thin line. The burly man that Ava didn't recognize flicked his anxious gaze between her and Luiz before finally settling on Ava.

With a voice edged with fear, he rasped, "You shouldn't be here."

6

Ava paused, trying to process his words. The flickering firelight cast eerie shadows on everyone's faces. Just like in the foyer, the small chandelier hanging from the ceiling was dark, and the room lacked any mounted candle sconces.

Determined not to appear speechless, Ava asked, "Well, I am here by invitation. Who are you?"

Before the man could respond, a loud, shrill voice rang out from behind Ava, "Well, hello darlings! Fancy seeing you all here. Cedric, still as fat as ever, I see. And Luiz, if my eyes don't deceive me, you've grown even more handsome. As for the rest of you…" Her voice trailed off, as if she couldn't muster the energy to continue. A second set of heavy footsteps followed closely behind her.

As the woman strode to the center of the room, Ava fought to keep her rage in check. She kept her head lowered, her straight, chocolate-brown hair swaying slightly with the effort. When the two newcomers stopped in the middle of the room, Ava felt the woman's gaze bore into her, as if it were piercing her very soul.

She clicked her tongue, amusement dripping from her voice. "Well, well, well, if it isn't Ava Collins. I trust you've moved on from the nanny business after everything that happened with Oliver." Her voice grated on Ava's nerves like nails on a chalkboard. Ava forced herself to meet the woman's gaze.

The newcomer was Edith Barkley, Oliver's aunt. She wore a flowing cobalt dress that hugged her curves and fell elegantly to her ankles. A diamond necklace glittered at her throat, catching the firelight with every slight movement. Her curly bronze hair, styled to frame her face, gave her a youthful appearance despite her age, with only a few wrinkles around her eyes hinting at the years gone by.

The man standing beside her, Brandon Alcott, nodded approvingly at Edith. His crisp, black suit fit his muscular frame perfectly, and his slicked-back, obsidian hair gleamed in the firelight. Ava braced herself, determined not to show any weakness to the wretched woman.

She managed a thin smile and adopted the sugary tone she used with clients. "Hello, Edith. I'd say it's a pleasure to see you, but that would be a lie. And I see you're still with Brandon. Tell me, when will you finally ditch that moron and go after someone who can form a full sentence?"

Edith's eyes sparked with anger, and Brandon started to open his mouth to respond, but she raised her slender hand to stop him. Out of the corner of her eye, Ava saw Luiz suppressing a laugh. The crackle of the fire seemed to quiet as Edith's gaze locked onto her.

With a cold, cruel smile, Edith said, "Do you ever think about what Oliver was feeling when he was kidnapped? I bet he was begging you to save him. He died with hope misplaced in you because you fell asleep. Oliver died because of you." Her words hit like a physical blow, knocking the breath from Ava's lungs. She shook uncontrollably, her vision blurred. Edith's triumphant smirk burned into her mind as Ava bolted from the living room.

Ava dashed toward the room across the foyer, flinging open the grand wooden doors. She fled into the refuge of the library. The cavernous room, once filled with the earthy, woody aroma of old books, now reeked of mildew and dust. The fireplace, which had been a cozy fixture in the corner, was dark and cold, its once-bright mantle now covered in cobwebs.

She made her way to one of the enormous bookshelves on her right, its dark mahogany stretching towards the ceiling. The books that once lined the shelves were now cloaked in a thick layer of dust, their spines peeling away from the pages.

As Ava moved among the stacks, her tears mingling with the dust swirling around her, she was overwhelmed by memories. She recalled countless rainy afternoons spent curled up in the leather armchairs, their once-soft cushions now worn and neglected. She and Oliver had spent hours absorbed in those books.

She remembered how Oliver was drawn to classics like *The Art of War* by Sun Tzu, *War and Peace* by Leo Tolstoy, and *The Republic* by Plato. While others might have found his choices unusual, Ava had always seen them as a testament to his unique intellect and depth. Now, those books seemed like distant echoes in the silent, dust-filled room.

She wiped her tears and headed for the exit, vowing not to let Edith's cruelty break her spirit. Ava had never liked Edith, not since their first encounter. She remembered Edith's disdainful attitude toward Oliver and her constant scorn for Hazel, his mother. Ava had always made an effort to keep Oliver distracted during

Edith's visits, which were frequent while Hazel's husband, Edward, was away on business.

As Ava neared the archway of the living room, she instinctively ducked into the shadows when she heard the muffled conversation from the other room.

Her heart pounded in her chest as she listened from her hidden spot.

Edith's voice, low and laced with frustration, whispered, "Would someone care to explain the threatening invitation I received in the mail?"

"I've been wondering about that myself. I have better things to do than be here." Luiz responded with a hint of exasperation.

Cedric's voice, barely above a whisper and quivering with fear, said, "This is judgment for what we did."

Edith scoffed dismissively, "That's absurd. No one but us knows what really happened to Oliver. Besides, we did the world a favor by getting rid of that budding psychopath."

Luiz cautiously suggested, "Maybe someone discovered our roles in his death and is seeking revenge."

Audrey cut in sharply, "Is this really something we should be discussing in front of Jocelyn? She had nothing to do with Oliver's death. She could turn us in."

A heavy silence fell before Edith finally said, "I wouldn't worry about her. She seems barely here, so I doubt she's been paying attention."

Brandon statedly arrogantly, "The reality is that no one outside of us knows how we made Oliver disappear. He's gone and we all know better than to talk about it with anyone else. Besides, even if she does threaten to report us, then I'll just get rid of her."

Terror sluiced through Ava as Brandon menacingly added, "I'll even kill that damned au pair if she becomes a problem."

7

Before Ava could step forward and demand answers, the manor's clock struck five; its chime echoing ominously through the silence like a herald of doom. The sudden hush in the room felt almost palpable, as if the house itself was holding its breath. Ava slipped back into the room, deliberately ignoring the icy stare from Edith.

Almost as if conjured by the tolling bell, a tall, wiry older man appeared at the edge of the room where the living and dining room converged. His butler's attire was immaculate, the black tailcoat and white cravat perfectly crisp, not a wrinkle in sight. The light from the fireplace cast a ghostly pallor on his already pale face, his sharp features etched with an expression of practiced detachment. A slight shiver ran through Ava as she took in the man's spectral appearance and the unsettling precision with which he moved.

He cleared his throat and announced, "Good evening. Thank you all for attending this special occasion. I'm Charles Walker, and I'll be your host for the evening." As he spoke, he swept his gaze over the assembled guests. "The organizer of this event prefers to remain anonymous, so I apologize for any inconvenience this may cause."

Cedric, leaning slightly forward in his chair and fixing his penetrating gaze on Charles, interjected smoothly, "My good man, it's a pleasure to meet you." He adjusted his posture, smoothing the front of his tailored jacket with a practiced hand. "I would ask who the organizer is, but I suspect I already know your answer. Instead, could you tell us anything about our mysterious host?"

Charles tilted his head thoughtfully, then straightened, his expression unwavering. "While I'm unable to disclose the identity of my master, I can share this: they are among you." His words hung in the air, and a tense silence settled over the room as everyone began to scrutinize one another.

Brandon strode towards the butler. His eyes narrowed, and his voice rang through the room, "I'm not in the mood for games. This place is creepy as hell, so why don't you just tell us who's really behind all this?"

To Ava's astonishment, Charles stood his ground, unfazed by Brandon's approach. "As I've said," He continued, his tone unruffled, "I cannot disclose any personal details about my employer. It's a matter you must unravel yourselves."

Brandon's face darkened with frustration as he reached toward Charles's shoulder, but before he could touch him, Luiz's calm voice cut through the charged air. "Hold on."

Brandon's hand froze mid-air, and he turned sharply to Luiz, his rage barely contained. "What did you just say?" he spat through clenched teeth. Ava couldn't help but notice the flicker of amusement on Edith's face as she watched the exchange.

Luiz, a smirk tugging at his lips, said nonchalantly, "I said wait. Let him talk. It's pretty clear he's not going to reveal who's behind this. The truth is, the person responsible is someone right here among us."

Brandon squinted at Luiz. "If it's so obvious, then who is it? Who summoned us all to this godforsaken manor?" He flung his arms out, his voice dripping with menace. "Which one of us is behind this twisted charade?"

Luiz pushed himself off the fireplace and sauntered over to Brandon. At around 5'9", Luiz was dwarfed by Brandon's imposing 6'2" frame. With a smirk, Luiz drawled, "I don't know who invited us all, but it certainly wasn't me. If it had been, I wouldn't have invited your ugly mug."

Brandon's eyes flared, and his fist rose, poised to strike. But before he could act, Charles cleared his throat sharply, stopping him.

His voice, though calm, carried an unmistakable authority. "Please, let's avoid violence. There will be consequences if you don't." Brandon's glare was met with Charles's unwavering gaze. "Now, if you'll all follow me to the dining room," he continued, turning on his heel and walking toward the door with deliberate steps, leaving no room for argument.

Ava quickly followed Charles into the dining room and was relieved to see that it remained unchanged. The room exuded a refined elegance that sharply contrasted with the library's neglected state.

At the heart of the room was a grand oak table, its rich, polished surface gleaming softly in the ambient light. The table's curved legs and intricate patterns spoke of craftsmanship and sophistication. Beneath it, an exquisite rug in muted tones stretched across the floor, adding warmth to the space.

Ava's eyes were drawn to the floor-to-ceiling bay windows on the left side of the room. Despite the grime clinging to the glass, the gray light filtering through cast a serene glow across the room. The multiple candle sconces mounted on the walls added a little light, their flickering flames creating shifting patterns of light and shadow.

On the table, each china plate was adorned with a neatly propped notecard, each one bearing a name and indicating a seat. Charles's voice broke the quiet, "Please find your name and take a seat. Dinner shall be served shortly."

As Ava reached her assigned seat, positioned next to the head of the table on the far side from the window, a heavy sense of unease settled over her, like a weight pressing down on her shoulders. Cedric sighed and dropped heavily into the chair to her left, while Luiz slid into the chair to her right with a predatory grace. The woman from the fire, who had not yet spoken, took her place across from Ava, with Audrey settling beside her.

Ava cast a glance down the length of the table, noting that Brandon had taken the head of the table with Edith to his left and Duncan to his right. The arrangement was as formal and deliberate as one would expect from a gathering with such undercurrents of hostility.

The room was thick with strained silence until the butlers began to stream in, their movements almost ghostly. Each butler, regardless of age or gender, shared that same unnerving pallor. Ava watched as they moved quietly, their steps barely audible on the polished floor.

The butlers, some elderly with stooped shoulders and others youthful with impassive expressions, carried large silver platters, their hands steady despite the weight they bore. They placed the platters down with a practiced precision, revealing an array of culinary delights. The clinking of cutlery and the soft rustle of serving dishes sang through the room as they served glasses of various wines alongside the food.

Ava's breath caught in her throat when she saw her plate, laden with her favorite dishes: slow-roasted honey glazed ham, golden and succulent; smoldering au gratin potatoes, bubbling and crisped to perfection; and buttery cornbread, its aroma promising comfort.

Even though Ava's mouth watered at the sight of her plate, she hesitated to eat. She glanced over at Luiz's plate, which was adorned with vibrant Paella Valenciana, jamón with steaming bread, and golden churros. His expression mirrored her own—a blend of hunger and unease. She noticed that everyone's plate was different, each one appearing to be a personal favorite.

It struck her with a chilling clarity: this almost felt like their final meal on death row.

Luiz's voice sliced through the room with a sharp edge, "Alright, whoever is behind this better come forward now. At first, the oddness was amusing, but this is crossing a line."

Cedric, looking puzzled, asked, "What do you mean? What's so strange about the food we've been served?"

Luiz's gaze swept across the table, his tone accusing, "Judging by everyone's reaction to their food, I'd bet that each of us was given our favorite meal. The real question is: how would someone know all of our favorite foods?"

Duncan chuckled weakly, "Maybe it was a lucky guess?"

Luiz's eyes narrowed thoughtfully. "I doubt it's that simple. This would likely require someone with personal knowledge of us or connections to uncover our favorite foods.." His gaze shifted pointedly to Edith and Brandon. "I'm leaning toward you two as the culprits. So, did you poison the food?"

Duncan nearly choked on his roast beef, gravy spilling from his mouth as he shot up in alarm. Edith, her face twisted into a smirk of feline amusement, responded, "We're as puzzled as the rest of you. If I wanted to kill you, trust me, poison wouldn't be my method." Brandon's grin widened as he cracked his knuckles.

Luiz ignored her comment and said to the table, "Since you'll not step forward, I promise you that before this evening is finished, I *will* find out who's behind this." Luiz's gaze remained locked on Edith's as he issued his challenge. His eyes blazed with a brazen determination.

Ava, her curiosity piqued, turned to Luiz. "So, what do you do in Spain? You mentioned you're a lawyer."

Luiz shifted his attention to her, his expression softening slightly. "Actually, I'm a prosecutor in Barcelona."

Ava's eyes widened with admiration. "That's amazing! I bet you've put away a lot of criminals."

Luiz's lips curved into a modest smile. "I have. I've made it my mission to clean up the streets by targeting drug dealers."

Ava nodded, clearly impressed. "That's a noble and worthy cause. I'm sure your parents must be proud."

A shadow crossed Luiz's caramel eyes, darkening them with an edge of bitterness. He leaned back slightly, his posture rigid. "My father was a deadbeat and my mother died a long time ago."

Ava responded softly, "I'm so sorry to hear that. But I'm sure your mother would be proud of how you turned out." She offered a gentle, understanding smile.

Luiz offered one of his own and returned to his food, his attention shifting away from the conversation. Ava turned to Cedric. "So, what do you do?"

Cedric's grin widened, his eyes twinkling with a mix of pride and mischief. "Well, my darling, I'm just a regular estate planning lawyer. Not quite as glamorous as Mr. Garcia's line of work, but it has its moments."

Ava tilted her head, feigning ignorance as she probed further. "If you wouldn't mind, could you explain what an estate planning lawyer does? And how did you come to work with Oliver's family, the Wellingtons?"

Cedric leaned back in his chair, his fingers lightly tapping his wine glass. "I help families create wills, designate beneficiaries, and handle the distribution of assets upon death. When Oliver was presumed dead, I assisted the Wellingtons with updating their will. And when they, unfortunately, passed away, I was responsible for enacting their final wishes."

Ava mentally filed away this piece of information, her mind already turning over the implications. "I see. Thank you for clarifying." She turned her attention to the woman with golden hair seated across from her. "So, what's your name and how did you come to be here?"

Her delicate, round face lifted from her half-eaten meal, and Ava was momentarily struck by the beauty of her emerald-green eyes, which seemed almost otherworldly. The woman spoke with a voice so gentle it could have been a whisper of wind. "My name is Jocelyn Cooper. I received an invitation like everyone else and found myself intrigued."

The name sparked a faint recognition at the edge of Ava's memory, like a distant echo. She pressed further, "And what's your connection to Oliver and his family?"

Jocelyn sighed, a faint trace of sadness flickering across her features. "Before Oliver disappeared, I was betrothed to him. It was an arrangement made by our families to enhance their wealth and status. Although I harbored no romantic feelings for him, I was deeply affected by his disappearance."

Ava's mind snapped into focus. She remembered the day Jocelyn was introduced to Oliver at the manor. The way they had seemed genuinely happy together, the blushes Jocelyn would have whenever Oliver presented her with flowers or recited poetry. It felt at odds with her claim of being platonic. Ava wondered to herself, If she didn't care for Oliver, then why the pretense of affection?

Questions churned in Ava's mind as she reflected on the unsettling conversation she had overheard earlier. What part did Cedric and Luiz play in Oliver's death? Why was Jocelyn present if she wasn't involved? Could Jocelyn be behind this as an act of revenge? How exactly did they kill Oliver? What was the purpose of this gathering? And what was that malevolent presence she had felt earlier?

As she pondered these questions, Ava absentmindedly picked at her food. She finally spoke up, her voice carrying a hint of melancholy, "I remember you now. I always thought you and Oliver made a lovely pair, and he was clearly quite taken with you."

Jocelyn took a measured sip of her red wine, her smile tinged with resignation. "Yes, he was. Although I never had any romantic feelings for him, he did become a good friend."

Sensing Jocelyn's reluctance to delve further into her past with Oliver, Ava turned her focus back to her meal. Silence descended over the table, punctuated only by the strained small talk that filled the void. It was evident from the exchanged glances and barely concealed animosity that everyone was eyeing each other with suspicion. As the light from the bay windows began to wane, the butlers glided in and quickly lit the candle sconces that lined the walls. The warm, flickering light cast an eerie glow over the room.

Ava's gaze flickered to Edith, who was smirking while engaged in quiet conversation with Brandon. Typical, she thought, that that wretched woman would find this whole situation amusing.

The meal was nearing its end when Duncan suddenly erupted, "Okay, I can't take it anymore. I need to know—did anyone else receive an invitation? Was there a threat if you didn't come?"

Ava's eyes widened at the bluntness of his question. She watched as Duncan, the former gardener for the Wellingtons, trembled slightly, his straight raven hair partially obscuring his anxious face. The room fell into an oppressive silence, each person seemingly waiting for someone to speak up. Ava finally broke the quiet, her voice steady despite her nerves, "I did. The letter threatened to kill my boyfriend if I didn't attend."

Jocelyn confessed softly, "I received a similar threat in my invitation." One by one, everyone except Edith and Brandon admitted to receiving a summons with a threat.

Luiz turned his piercing gaze toward the pair, "And what about you two?"

They both grinned, and Edith said with a touch of mockery, "As a matter of fact, both Brandon and I received invitations. I'm curious when the real fun will begin because this has been dreadfully dull."

Suddenly, the ghostly butlers swept into the room, taking positions behind each person. Ava's heart pounded as she saw them draw sleek pistols, each one now trained on a guest. She didn't have to turn to know that there was a barrel pointed at her skull.

The head butler moved into the room and positioned himself at the end of the table closest to the window. The candles flickered violently, casting monstrous, writhing shadows on the walls. The room's warmth evaporated, replaced by a creeping chill that slithered down Ava's spine.

She glanced around the table. Everyone except for her, Duncan, Cedric, and Jocelyn remained unperturbed, their faces masks of indifference.

Charles cleared his throat. "I trust your meal was to your liking. I'm sure you're all eager to know why you're here. I'll explain shortly, but before I do, you should know that one of you will die after my explanation. I suggest you remain still and listen carefully."

8

Ava's heart plummeted, and she struggled to breathe as Charles's ominous words sank in. Panic threatened to overwhelm her, but she forced herself to look around the room, seeking something to anchor her thoughts. Her mind fixated on the memory of Carter's face, his warmth, and the comfort of his presence, imagining them as a refuge amidst the chaos.

She touched the ring on her finger; its cool metal a small but reassuring reminder of him. With each breath, she steadied herself, her heartbeat gradually returning to a more manageable rhythm. As the panic receded, Ava refocused on her surroundings, determined not to let fear break her.

Duncan and Jocelyn were visibly shaking, their faces ashen and eyes wide with terror. Duncan's hands gripped the edge of the table so tightly that his knuckles turned white, while Jocelyn's quivering lip betrayed her fear despite her attempt to hold herself together. Cedric sat slack-jawed, his gaze locked in horror on the butler looming behind Brandon. Beads of sweat were beginning to form on his bushy brows, and his hands twitched involuntarily.

Brandon and Luiz, on the other hand, were a stark contrast. Both wore heavy scowls, their eyes cold and menacing. Brandon's fingers drummed impatiently on the table, a vein throbbing in his temple, while Luiz's jaw was set with an icy determination, his gaze locked onto Charles as if willing him to crumble to dust.

Audrey, in her usual detached manner, wore a deep frown that seemed almost casual given the gravity of the situation. Her expression was the same one she might use for a minor inconvenience, as though the unfolding drama were nothing more than a minor disruption to her evening. Ava couldn't help but wonder if Audrey ever showed any emotion other than annoyance.

Lastly, Ava turned her gaze to Edith. The woman's delicate, manicured hand was pressed to her mouth, though she was struggling to stifle her mirth. As Edith let out a sharp, shrieking cackle, her red nails caught the flickering candlelight, casting shifting hues across her fingers. Her laughter was a jagged sound, so grating that Ava felt an urge to claw at her ears to escape the noise.

"Finally, things get interesting," Edith announced, her demeanor shifting from amused to frantic. Her eyes glinted with a wild fervor, and spittle flew from her mouth as she raged on, "I hope you can follow through on your threats. Don't forget it was I who orchestrated Oliver's demise. I swear, when I discover who's behind this, I'll kill you!"

Her tirade was abruptly halted by the thunderous slam of Luiz's fists on the table. The wood shuddered under the force of his strike, sending a ripple of silence through the room as everyone's attention snapped to him.

As Luiz slowly rose to his feet, his face a mask of raw fury, he growled, "I don't know who the hell you think you are, but—" His words were abruptly cut short by the sharp crack of the gun's butt against his temple. Gasps erupted around the table as he crumpled onto the surface, blood trickling from his head and pooling beneath him. He tried to lift his head defiantly, but his body remained motionless, slumped in his chair.

Charles's gaze swept over the table, his features wrinkled with contempt as though he were surveying a collection of bothersome insects. "Now that you've gotten that out of your system," he said coolly, "I trust you're ready to listen." He paused, allowing the weight of his words to settle. "As I mentioned earlier, I will now explain why you are all here. Each of you received an invitation to this dinner. The terms were clear: refuse to attend, and your most guarded secrets would be exposed to the public, destroying your reputations and lives. The reason you are here tonight is to face judgment for your roles in the disappearance and subsequent death of Oliver Wellington."

The air thickened as everyone absorbed Charles's chilling proclamation. Ava's mind raced, and her stomach churned with nausea. It dawned on her that someone was blaming her for Oliver's disappearance, though all she had done was fall asleep. How could that possibly be a crime?

Charles broke the quiet with a measured tone, "While it would be simple to end your lives now, my master is merciful and has granted you a chance to survive—well, except for one of you. You have until morning to uncover the evidence of your secrets hidden somewhere in this manor. If you succeed, you may leave here alive. If you fail to uncover the evidence of your crimes, you will die." He paused, letting the weight of his words settle over them. "To prove the validity of my master's claims, one of you must perish, and your secret will be laid bare."

Charles's icy gaze shifted to Cedric, whose face had drained of color. "Cedric Crawford," Charles began, his tone like a blade, "for years, you've been subtly altering wills, skimming estates from the grieving without their knowledge. Your deceit amassed you considerable wealth. But now, it's time to account for your role in Oliver Wellington's disappearance."

The butler's gaze then turned to Edith, his expression darkening. "Before Edith and Brandon took Oliver, she came to you with a proposition: once his parents updated their will, you were to alter it so that Edith would inherit the estate. What was meant for charity instead lined your pockets, all for a handsome sum."

Charles's head swung back to Cedric, his stare as cold and unforgiving as death itself. "You knew of the crime planned against Oliver and chose to do nothing. You watched his parents suffer in silence, and still, you did nothing. Your greed has sealed your fate. Your meal was poisoned, leaving you with mere minutes before death claims you. I suggest you use that time to seek solace with your maker."

9

Charles turned on his heel and walked out of the room, the rest of the staff gliding out behind him. Ava could feel the malevolent presence lurking at the edge of her consciousness, as if it were watching her every move. The sudden warmth of the room felt suffocating, as if she were trapped in a baking oven, and her soft cotton dress clung to her skin like coarse sandpaper.

Before Ava could succumb to the rising tide of hysteria, the shock among the others began to dissolve. The room erupted into a flurry of activity and frantic whispers as everyone struggled to process the chilling revelation and the grim reality of their situation.

Cedric's face was streaked with tears, his voice shaking, "I'm not going to die, am I? Surely, Charles was just jesting!"

Brandon, his face a mask of fury, roared, "Whoever's behind this needs to come forward now! I swear I'll…"

In the chaos of overlapping voices, Ava's gaze fell on Luiz. He stood apart from the turmoil, his expression one of an approaching storm. A muscle twitched in his jaw as he suddenly slammed his fists onto the table with such force that glasses rattled and silverware clattered.

"EVERYBODY, QUIET!" he thundered, cutting through the cacophony like a knife. The room fell into stunned silence.

Luiz took a deep breath and sighed, "It's pointless to turn on each other without any concrete evidence. What just happened was horrific, but we need to keep our heads if we're going to get through this."

Audrey's voice rang out, sharp and practical, "Then what do you suggest we do? If Charles was telling the truth, then someone here is responsible for Cedric's impending death."

Cedric's face drained of color as he listened, a look of sheer dread etched on his features. Luiz rubbed his stubbled chin absently, his eyes darting around the room. "I propose we wait," he said steadily. "At this point, all we have are threatening invitations and the cryptic words of a butler. If Cedric dies, it confirms that our invitations and our host's claims are real. It would mean that someone among us has orchestrated this twisted game of torture and death. If he survives, then it suggests that the threats were merely intended to scare us into submission."

To Ava's surprise, Jocelyn's voice was soft but firm as she asked, "If Cedric does die, how do we know you aren't behind this?"

Luiz's eyes narrowed as he considered her question. His thin brows furrowed in concentration before he replied, "It's not a perfect defense, but it's worth considering. If I were orchestrating this, wouldn't it be wiser for me to stay silent and avoid drawing attention? As the only one that is a criminal prosecutor, why would I risk exposing myself as the mastermind behind all of this?"

Though his logic seemed sound, Edith, Brandon, and Audrey exchanged wary glances, their distrust evident. They scrutinized Luiz, their skepticism clear.

Meanwhile, Cedric sat slumped over, his usually ruddy face now a sickly green. Sweat beaded on his forehead and dripped down his face, mingling with the remnants of his meal. His lips were dry and cracked. The fear in his eyes was unmistakable; he gasped for breath, his movements jerky and desperate as he glanced around the room.

Cedric panted, his breath coming in ragged bursts, "You all aren't going to believe that mysterious chap, are you? I'm telling you I'm fine!" His plea was met with a heavy silence as everyone watched him, their eyes wide and unblinking. Ava felt as if the room itself was a coiled spring, poised to snap.

He began to wheeze and frantically rubbed at his chest, his movements growing increasingly frenzied. "Must be acid reflux from the meal and the stress from everything," he managed to gasp out, his voice barely above a whisper.

With a final, desperate attempt to reassure them, Cedric rasped, "I'm telling you I'm fi—" His words were cut short as he clutched at his chest, his body convulsing violently in his chair. Ava's eyes widened in horror as his pupils bulged and he began to froth at the mouth.

Terror seized Cedric's face, turning it a ghastly shade of blue. His hands clawed at his neck, gasping for breath, but only wet, choking sounds escaped him. The scene was grotesque, and Ava was overwhelmed by the realization that witnessing a man's death felt like an interminable, nightmarish eternity.

Eventually, Cedric's convulsions halted. His body slumped back against the chair, mouth agape in a silent scream, eyes wide and frozen in a final expression of horror. Her stomach churned, her throat tight with the urge to scream or flee, while tears streamed down her face.

Jocelyn's voice, soft yet tinged with dread, cut through the hushed room. "Is that going to happen to us?" Her question hung in the air, unanswered by the silent stares of the others, save for Duncan, whose tears flowed freely as he wept quietly.

Luiz took a moment to collect his thoughts before speaking, his gaze sharp and focused. "I doubt it. This—" he gestured toward Cedric's lifeless body with a grim expression, "—is likely just the beginning. I believe the mastermind behind this has more elaborate plans for the rest of us."

Audrey, her voice like ice, demanded, "What do you mean? Are you suggesting that one of us is planning on killing everyone here? For what purpose would that serve?"

Luiz met her gaze evenly, "That is precisely what I'm suggesting. There are, in my view, two potential explanations for the situation we find ourselves in. First, one of us might be orchestrating these deaths to cover up their involvement in Oliver's disappearance. They could be eliminating witnesses or eliminating those who know too much. Second, there might be an external force at play—someone seeking retribution for the death of Oliver, and they are using us as a means to exact their revenge."

He continued, his tone becoming more resolute, "Given the manner in which Cedric died, it's clear that the methods of death will vary. It's not just a simple act of murder; it's a methodical and deliberate process designed to instill fear and confusion. We might face different forms of demise, each tailored to our perceived sins or weaknesses. The mastermind's aim is likely to inflict maximum psychological torment as well as physical harm."

The weight of Luiz's words hung in the air emphasizing the stark reality that each of them could face a different, equally horrific fate. The realization that their tormentor might have meticulously planned out their deaths only deepened the sense of dread within Ava's being.

Edith's laughter through the space. "That's preposterous!" she sneered, her tone dripping with scorn. "I've already said that no one else knew what we did. Who would have cared enough about him to want revenge?"

Her gaze flickered to Ava and Jocelyn with a cold, assessing look. Ava's thoughts were a whirlwind, her eyes fixated on the grotesque sight of Cedric's lifeless, bloated body. How can they forget that there's a corpse right here? What are we even doing at this table?

Before Edith could launch another verbal assault, Duncan bolted upright, his face pale and eyes wide with raw fear. He was practically vibrating with panic. "What are we still doing here?" he yelled, his voice cracking with desperation. "Someone just died! I don't care about the threats anymore, I'm leaving right now."

Without waiting for a response, Duncan turned and dashed out of the room. The sound of his rapid footsteps echoed in the house, abruptly interrupted by a heart-wrenching cry. "No, no, no, no, no! Please let me out!"

She stole a glance at Luiz. Concern briefly flashed across his face as he pushed himself away from the table. With a deliberate calm, he slid his hands into his pockets and sauntered towards the foyer. Just before crossing the threshold into the living room, he paused, a hint of a smile playing on his lips. "Aren't the rest of you coming?" he called out, his tone laced with a careful nonchalance. "I wouldn't suggest you stay alone right now."

Jocelyn and Ava exchanged a knowing look, understanding flashing in her emerald eyes. Without hesitation, they both rose and followed Luiz's steady footsteps.

As they stepped into the dimly lit living room, Ava heard Edith murmur to Brandon and Audrey. Their hurried footsteps followed behind her. The neglected fire's feeble glow cast flickering shadows that crept and writhed along the walls.

Upon entering the foyer, Ava found Duncan frantically pounding on the door. Luiz approached him with a detached demeanor. As Duncan's fist came down for another strike, Luiz effortlessly caught it mid-swing, his grip firm and unyielding.

"What's the matter?" Luiz's voice was unruffled, his tone almost clinical.

Duncan spun around, yanking his hand from Luiz's grasp. His breathing was ragged, and Ava thought he resembled a frightened animal trapped in a corner. Without warning, he erupted into manic laughter, his eyes wide with hysteria.

"What's the matter?" Duncan's voice cracked as he laughed. "I've been dragged to this bizarre dinner party with people I never wanted to see again. I had a gun pointed at my head, watched a man die, and now you lunatics are acting like nothing happened as you discuss—"

Before Duncan could finish, Luiz moved with a swift motion. A flash of movement, and Duncan's head jerked sideways as he crumpled to the floor. Luiz grabbed him roughly by the collar and hauled him upright.

"Pull yourself together, Duncan," Luiz snarled, his voice low and threatening. He shoved Duncan towards the door, his frustration barely contained. Muttering something in Spanish under his breath, he added, "Now, tell us what's wrong and why you were slamming on the door."

The abrupt shift in Luiz's demeanor left everyone in silence.

Duncan gingerly touched the blood trickling from his nose and winced, his face contorted in pain. "I was trying to leave," he grumbled, "but the doors are locked."

Luiz's lips curled into a small, satisfied smile. "Thank you for that. Let me take a look at the door."

As Luiz examined it, peering through the window panes bordered with intricate ironwork, Ava scanned the rest of the group. Audrey sat with an air of indifferent boredom, idly inspecting her nails. Jocelyn, on the other hand, looked as though she might collapse at any moment. Her face was ghostly white, eyes wide and glassy.

Brandon and Edith, whispering to each other, kept casting furtive glances towards Luiz. Edith's gaze shifted abruptly towards Ava, a cruel, malevolent smile stretching across her lips. Brandon, catching on to Edith's intent, followed suit. His mud-brown eyes and sharply angular face were twisted into a similar, unsettling grin. Ava tried to keep her composure, but the intensity of their gazes made her hands shake slightly.

Luiz's voice broke the grim quiet. "I'll be back in a moment. I need to check something in the living room."

After a brief, tense minute, Luiz reentered the foyer, his expression somber. "It seems Duncan was correct. The doors are indeed chained shut. Most likely, the other exits are similarly secured."

Brandon, his patience fraying, snapped, "Well? What else is there? You clearly have more to say."

Luiz sighed, his broad shoulders rising and falling with the effort. "It appears that a couple of the butlers from dinner are stationed outside, likely armed with the same guns they threatened us with. In essence, if we attempt to escape before morning, they'll most likely shoot us on sight. For the time being, we're effectively locked inside this manor."

10

Luiz suggested, "How about we head back to the living room and talk this over? Standing around isn't getting us anywhere. And besides…" His eyes flicked to Ava, Duncan, and Jocelyn, all visibly shaken. "I think some of us need to sit down and process what just happened." One-by-one, they followed Luiz.

Ava sank into the plush, velvet armchair to the left of the fire, the warmth of the flames licking at her chilled skin. The entryway to the dining room was just to her right, and the foyer lay behind her. The softness of the chair enveloped her weary frame, and she shivered slightly as exhaustion set in.

Luiz, ever the pragmatic leader, tossed a few logs onto the dying fire, sending a shower of sparks into the hearth. He leaned casually against the mantle, scanning the room with a mix of caution and resolve.

Across from her, Edith and Brandon loomed near the fireplace. Duncan and Jocelyn had settled onto the sofa positioned next to Ava's chair. Audrey occupied the armchair on the other side of the sofa.

Edith snapped, her voice dripping with menace. "Is this the moment when whoever is behind this finally steps forward? I assure you, if you come forward now, no harm will come to you."

When no one stepped forward, Audrey's voice cut through the room. "How do we know it isn't you behind this? You've been adamant that one of us is the culprit since you arrived."

Before Edith could interject, Luiz's voice interrupted, "As far as I can tell, everyone here is a suspect. Each of you has motives for wanting to see the rest of us dead."

Ava's breath caught in her throat, a sharp pang of disbelief and confusion shooting through her. Her mind raced, a tumult of panic and frustration. Her voice wavered but grew louder, "Why would you think I'd want to kill any of you? Do I look like I have the means or the ability to orchestrate something like this?" Her voice sharpened, the undercurrent of anger and helplessness rising like a tide. "My boyfriend was threatened to force me here tonight. I've been lying to him all week, and it's been driving me insane!"

She whirled to face Luiz, her eyes blazing with annoyance. "And you? I don't even know who you are!

So why, on earth, would I want to kill you when I've never met you before?"

Luiz tilted his head, a curious expression flickering across his face. "You mean you truly don't know the real story behind Oliver's disappearance?"

Ava's anger boiled over. "No, I don't! I've been confused since I arrived, and you all seem to be implicated in what happened to Oliver." She turned her fiery gaze on Edith. "What did you do to him?"

Edith, fingers idly twisting one of her curls, flashed a heartless smile. "Oh, I don't think I'll tell you. It's far more amusing to watch you squirm in ignorance. And besides, I'd gain nothing from revealing it." The cruel satisfaction in Brandon's harsh expression confirmed that Ava wouldn't find any answers from him either.

Jocelyn, her emerald eyes wide with distress, spoke up. "I think it's fair to assume that neither Ava nor I are behind this. We have no reason to be involved."

Audrey's gaze shifted to Jocelyn, her tone unyielding. "I agree that Ava isn't behind this, but you're still under suspicion. We all received threats tied to our secrets and reputations. Ava's the only one who didn't."

Jocelyn's cheeks flushed a deep red. "But I don't know what happened to Oliver! I have no motive for revenge."

Audrey's eyes narrowed. "That's not entirely accurate. Gossip travels, especially among staff of prominent families. You might know more than you're letting on." Jocelyn looked mortified, her fingers gripping the edge of the armrest tightly.

Ava, desperate to change the topic for Jocelyn's sake, asked, "What did Charles mean about our secrets being in this house?" The room fell into a contemplative silence, each person lost in thought.

Brandon, his broad shoulders stiffening, finally spoke. "Maybe I should search around and find out." He draped an arm around Edith's shoulders, casting a glance down at her with a smirk. "Perhaps it's hidden in one of the bedrooms upstairs." He winked at Edith and began to head for the stairs in the foyer.

Edith chuckled, her lips curling into a scheming smile. "Hmm, maybe we should search all the rooms just to be thorough."

As Brandon and Edith's footsteps dwindled on the stairs, Luiz's voice cut through the silence, soft yet heavy with warning. "I'd stay away from them if I were you. I understand if you don't trust me, but be cautious. I've been uneasy since I stepped foot in this house, and I'm not easily intimidated." With a final glance at them all, he turned on his heel and walked back toward the dining room.

Audrey stood and stretched her slim figure. She wore a mask of boredom as she addressed the remaining trio. "I don't think you three are behind this, and it would be a pity for young people like yourselves to meet an early end. So, be careful." She said, her tone icy and indifferent, before making her way toward the dining room.

After Audrey's departure, Duncan breathed, "I can't believe this nightmare is happening." He wiped away tears as he shuffled with a heavy tread toward the stairs.

Ava's gaze shifted to Jocelyn, who remained motionless, her eyes fixed on the fire with a vacant expression. Ava's heart ached at the sight of her, and her own fear surged as she contemplated Duncan's haunting words. The nightmare, she realized, was only just beginning.

11

Ava turned toward Jocelyn, the firelight gilding her soft, round face with a warm, golden hue. The flames danced in her deep, evergreen eyes, like an inferno consuming a lush forest. Despite the chaos that had unfolded, not a single strand of her cascading, golden hair was out of place. Ava marveled at how gracefully she had grown from the gangly teen she remembered.

Ava, in stark contrast, looked worn and frazzled. Her auburn hair, once meticulously styled, now tumbled in disarray around her face, with strands escaping their pins and falling into her eyes. The flickering firelight accentuated the shadows under her eyes, highlighting the fatigue etched into her features. Her soft, cotton dress, which had once been a comfort, now felt abrasive and heavy against her skin.

Not wanting to linger in the silence, Ava said, "You know, even though we're being hunted by a deranged psychopath, I'm glad I got to see you. You've grown into such a beautiful woman." When Jocelyn remained quiet, Ava continued, "I never thought I'd be back here."

She sighed deeply and said, "Being here brings back so many memories." Her gaze grew distant as she looked at the center of the room. "On cold nights, Oliver and I would play cards or board games right next to the fire. Sometimes, I'd make us hot cocoa and we'd listen to Christmas music on the radio."

Tears welled up in her eyes, shimmering like the last glints of sunlight before dusk. "I always loved him like a little brother. He was such a sweet and caring kid."

Jocelyn turned to Ava, her eyes shadowed with sadness. "He wasn't as sweet as you remember him."

Ava felt a shiver creep down her spine, her voice barely more than a whisper. "What do you mean?" The shadows in the room seemed to thicken and deepen, closing in around them.

Jocelyn's delicate hands clenched tightly in her lap. "When we were alone, he'd try to make advances on me." Her voice filled with emotion and tears brimmed her eyes, "He'd try to touch me and when I would refuse, he'd threaten me." The shadows on the walls seemed to writhe and twist, as if relishing the unfolding story.

Ava was stunned. The boy she had always seen as sweet and innocent now seemed a lie. Her mind faltered, words escaping her grasp, but Jocelyn continued, her voice heavy with anguish. "When he wasn't trying to take advantage of me, he'd spew vile things about the staff—his tutors, the gardener, the maid, even his parents."

Ava felt something within her shatter, the pieces falling away. She wanted to deny it, but Jocelyn's tear-streaked face was devoid of deceit. A roar filled Ava's mind, her body trembling with the force of it. How had she missed this? Had her affection for him blinded her to his true nature? Had he deceived her into believing he was good? Were any of the moments she'd shared with Oliver genuine?

Ava's head swam with a torrent of questions. She buried her face in her hands, hair falling over her fingers, obscuring her eyes. Her voice emerged as a pained croak. "Why was he like that?"

Jocelyn exhaled a heavy sigh, her hands clutching the armrests of her chair. "Some would say it was his nature. Others might blame his parents' absence. But I believe it was the house."

Ava raised her head, her eyes meeting Jocelyn's with a mix of confusion and desperation. "What do you mean?"

Jocelyn's gaze grew distant. "You must have felt it too. This place feels wrong, almost as if it harbors a deep-seated malevolence. Even the land seems tainted by a dark... presence."

Ava's thoughts drifted back to her arrival, to that unsettling sense of being watched by something otherworldly. Yet, something about Jocelyn's explanation didn't fully align. She leaned forward, her voice tight with curiosity. "How and why do you think this presence affected Oliver?"

Jocelyn's eyes flitted to the fire, her expression pained and solemn. "There could be a curse on the land, or perhaps a demon has taken root here. I'm not sure. But what I do know is that everyone in Oliver's family who lived here or spent significant time in this estate became corrupted. They all turned wicked."

Ava shook her head. "That can't be true! Both of his parents were kind and generous people."

Jocelyn's face was marked by a sadness that seemed to stretch beyond the room's shadows, her fingers nervously twisting the fabric of her dress.

Jocelyn's voice was heavy with sorrow as she continued, "Were they, though? Oliver's father was barely present during his upbringing, and there were whispers of extensive affairs involving both of his parents. I even heard that Mr. Wellington fathered a child in another country. I've heard that even Edith was a much kinder person until she started spending significant time here. My parents recall rumors of Oliver's grandparents' rottenness as well, though I never knew them personally. There's a tale that this corruption has tainted the Wellington family for generations."

The weight of Jocelyn's words left Ava stunned into silence. Her mind whirled with the revelations, her stomach churning with a mix of disbelief and unease. Jocelyn's gentle hand, manicured and delicate, covered Ava's with a comforting warmth. Her voice was soft, soothing amidst the chaos. "I know this is overwhelming, but I want you to understand that Oliver did truly care for you. Despite his harsh words about everyone else, he never spoke ill of you."

A wave of relief washed over Ava, the truth in Jocelyn's words a balm to her broken heart. She nodded, her voice steady despite the turmoil inside her. "Thank you. That means a lot to me." Eager to shift the focus away from her own grief, she asked, "If I may be so bold, why are you here? What secret are you hiding?"

Jocelyn rose from her chair with a fluid grace, every movement deliberate and poised. Her ruby gown hugged her subtle curves and slender frame, the hem skimming her ankles and revealing the onyx heels that peeked out with each step. Ava couldn't help but marvel at how Jocelyn had blossomed into her beauty, recognizing that once she fully realized her potential, she would undoubtedly become one of the most desired women in England.

A shadow of sorrow crossed Jocelyn's face as she whispered, "My secret is that I was in love." Without elaborating further, she turned and made her way towards the library, her departure leaving Ava alone with the heavy burden of new truths and lingering questions about the boy she had loved.

The Killer

12

As I rounded the corner into the kitchen, the sound of my prey rummaging through the silver drawers reached me. My heartbeat pounded in my ears, and a fiery sensation spread through my body. The house seemed to hum with a restless, pulsating energy.

The handle of my razor-sharp knife felt slick with the sweat of my palms. Despite months of meticulous planning and practice, nothing could match the raw intensity of this moment. I had prepared for this for so long. Tonight, it was time for them to pay. Tonight was about retribution.

The ghostly whispers from the house began as mere murmurs, but as I silently approached my unsuspecting target, they grew louder and more frantic. They whispered horrible, malicious things, speaking of ancient secrets and the dark truths these people tried to keep hidden. The voices wound through my body, but I was unafraid; I had already succumbed to their influence long ago.

The woman remained oblivious as I loomed silently behind her. I raised a hand and gently tapped her slim shoulders. The whispers in the house swelled into a frantic crescendo, pressing in around me.

When she finally turned, her face was etched with sheer terror. I flashed a predatory grin, watching as fear overtook her, making her tremble uncontrollably.

She stammered, "B-b-but, why a-and h-how-"

Before she could finish her sentence, I covered her mouth with my hand. I seethed, "Wouldn't you like to know, but unfortunately for you, you never will."

Without warning, I drove my knife into her lungs and twisted, a loud crunch echoed in the room. She bucked and tried to bite my hand, but I slammed her head into the cabinet behind her. Warm blood oozed over my hand from her torso, but not as much as I expected.

I leaned in close and whispered, "As much as I would love to stay and torture you, I do have to stick to a tight schedule." With a squelching sound, I removed the knife and aimed for her neck. She squealed and kicked out her legs, but I easily overpowered her.

With lethal precision, I drew my knife across her jugular and crimson blood sprayed out. Her eyes were wide as she tried to cover her mangled throat. She attempted to scream for help, but she couldn't make a sound.

Her movements slowed and then ceased entirely. I let out a sigh, frustrated that I couldn't prolong her suffering. Grabbing one of her limp hands, I placed it on the counter and muttered to myself, "Well, time to get to work."

13

Ava had lost track of how long she'd been sitting alone by the fire, her hands warmed by the flickering flames. She guessed it had been around thirty minutes since Jocelyn had left. Her thoughts churned relentlessly, replaying the chaotic events that had unfolded since her arrival. The questions assaulted her mind with no clear answers in sight.

Who had invited them all here? Could someone in the group be the killer? Why, if she had no secrets, had she been summoned? What exactly happened to Oliver, and what part did these people play in his disappearance?

Frustrated by the barrage of unanswered questions, she rose from her chair, stretching her stiff limbs. She ran her fingers through her shoulder-length brown hair, smoothing out the knots. As she stretched her arms and legs, the light from the fire cast a warm glow on her olive skin.

Ava was relieved she had opted for a comfortable sundress instead of one of the clingy numbers she usually reserved for work or special occasions with Carter. She wandered over to the mirror at the back of the living room and took stock of her reflection.

Tonight had aged her like nothing else ever had. As she studied her reflection, her fingers nervously toyed with the ring on her left hand, twisting it back and forth. The ring, a small token from Carter, was the only piece of normalcy left in this chaotic night, and she clung to it as a fleeting comfort amidst the uncertainty.

She sighed and strode back towards the fire, but jumped when she heard a blood-curdling scream emanating from beyond the dining room. Without thinking, Ava hurdled for the dining room and aimed for the door to the kitchen at the back of the room. When she entered the kitchen, she stopped dead in her tracks.

Ruby blood coated the room. The floor, the kitchen island, the countertops, the cabinets, and the steel cookware hanging from a rack that hovered over the island, dripped with it. What was usually a pristine and shining kitchen, full of gray marble and similarly colored cabinets of oak, had become ravaged with the stain of blood and bits of gore. The stench of death and iron stuffed itself inside Ava's nose so deeply that she thought she was going to vomit.

When she located the source of the scream, she almost collapsed from shock. Jocelyn was sobbing next to Audrey, the former maid, who was slumped on the floor and had a deep gash across her throat. Blood still slowly oozed from her neck and her face was still contorted in the shape of a terrible shriek.

Ava thought the scene couldn't be any worse until she saw Audrey's hands. Whoever killed her had cut off her hands and placed them on the counter. Ava's stomach roiled as she noticed that each hand had been stabbed to the counter with a silver knife.

Her mind reeled, struggling to make sense of the horrific sight before her. The chaos and blood seemed to defy logic. Ava turned to Jocelyn, who was crouched on the floor, her sobs muffled by the strands of her disheveled hair. "What happened? Did you see anything?"

Jocelyn's voice was choked with distress as she replied, her hair clinging to her tear-streaked face, "No, I didn't. I just came in and found her like this."

As Ava absorbed the scene, she heard rapid footsteps approaching. Luiz burst into the kitchen, his eyes sweeping the gruesome tableau with a steely, impassive gaze. His calm demeanor set Ava on edge.

With furrowed brows, Luiz turned his attention to Jocelyn and asked, "What happened here?"

She replied shakily, "I just came in and found her like this. I swear, I don't know what happened."

"And why should I believe you? It's possible you killed her and only screamed to cover your tracks."

Jocelyn's mouth worked soundlessly, her eyes wide with panic. Ava cut in sharply, "You have no right to accuse her. If anyone should be questioned, it's you."

Luiz raised an eyebrow, a smirk tugging at his lips. "Oh, really? And why's that?"

Ava met his gaze firmly. "Because you were the last person known to see Audrey alive. After you went into the dining room, she followed shortly after. Jocelyn was with me in the living room and only left to go to the library after you did."

He blanched at Ava's accusation, but before he could respond, Duncan burst into the room, Edith and Brandon hot on his heels. "What hap—"

Ava interrupted, her voice sharp with irritation, "Jocelyn found her like this. She didn't see anything and she's not the killer."

Edith sidestepped Duncan with a smirk. "Well, isn't this a twist? It's about time that little thief got what was coming to her."

14

Ava's gaze hardened as she turned to Edith, her eyes narrowing. "What do you mean by that? No one deserves this."

Edith's lips curled into a mocking smile. "You really don't know?" She flicked one of her slender wrists dismissively. "Oh, well. I suppose it can't be helped. That woman often swiped silver from my sister and her husband."

Ava folded her arms tightly, her expression a mixture of disbelief and anger. "No. No way. She wouldn't do that to the Wellingtons. You're lying…" Her voice trailed off as something caught her eye. She pivoted towards the silver drawer and moved swiftly to it.

Jocelyn's voice was a soft murmur of confusion. "What are you doing, Ava?" Ava ignored her, her focus locked on the drawer. She forced herself to sift through the blood-smeared silverware, trying to keep her nausea at bay.

Her hands shook as she pulled out crumpled wads of paper. Luiz moved in closer, peering over her shoulder. He mumbled, "Now, what do we have here?" A faint scent of cedar and sage drifted from him, mingling with the metallic tang of blood.

Duncan asked impatiently, "Well? What are they?"

Ava exhaled sharply. "They appear to be receipts from various pawn shops across London." She turned her gaze back to Edith. "How did you know about this?"

Edith shrugged nonchalantly. "I caught her in the act years ago. I happened to walk into the kitchen one day and saw that little thief shoving silver utensils into her uniform."

Ava's anger flared. "Why didn't you tell the Wellingtons?"

Edith's smile twisted into something crueler, her eyes glinting with malice. "Because it was far more entertaining to threaten her, of course." She let out a cruel laugh, her short curls bouncing with each chuckle.

Ava's hands trembled, her vision blurring with fiery rage. "You're truly a wretched woman," she spat, her voice thick with venom. "If another life is lost, I hope it's yours."

A stunned silence blanketed the room. Duncan, Jocelyn, and even Luiz were caught off guard by Ava's outburst. But Brandon and Edith remained unfazed, their smug smiles stretching even wider.

Brandon's voice dripped with mockery. "Well, well, look at that. It seems she's finally grown some claws."

Before Ava could lunge at them, her fury barely contained, Luiz's voice stopped her. "Enough," he commanded, his voice low and firm. His muscles tensed as he furrowed his brows. "We don't have time for this. If you're done here, we should return to the living room."

Edith's voice dripped with sarcasm. "Oh, and why should we follow you? Planning to off us all at once to finish this charade?"

Luiz's gaze was steely as he crossed his arms, the room thick with unspoken threats. After a heartbeat of silence, he replied, "None of us need to linger beside a corpse."

She covered her mouth in mock surprise and teased, "Luiz, don't tell me you're getting squeamish around dead bodies. I thought with your... job, you'd be used to this sort of thing."

His eyes flared with warning, and his harsh expression grew more menacing by the second. Ava could see, from his reaction, that Edith's comment was aimed at more than just his role as a prosecutor. She tucked it away to ask Luiz later.

Ignoring the argument between Luiz and Edith, Ava turned her gaze back to Audrey. She glanced at the gash on her neck. Despite her distaste for the woman, she wouldn't wish such a fate on anyone. As she prepared to turn back to the heated argument among Brandon, Edith, and Luiz, something caught her eye—something was missing.

Ava cut through their quarrel, "Hey, something's missing from Audrey."

Luiz turned sharply, his brow furrowed in confusion, "What do you mean?"

Ava pointed to Audrey's neck, her voice tight, "Her necklace is missing." She recalled seeing the silver locket from earlier in the evening.

Luiz frowned, clearly puzzled. "Are you certain she was wearing a necklace? I don't remember her having one."

To Ava's surprise, Edith chimed in, a hint of smugness in her tone. "Yes, she did have a necklace—a locket, in fact." She flashed a thin smile at Ava, "Good eye, detective."

Jocelyn, her voice barely above a whisper, asked, "What was in it?"

Edith's expression softened briefly. "It held a photo of her late husband and their young daughter."

Jocelyn only nodded, and Ava took a moment to think before speaking. "We should check Cedric's body," she suggested. "If something was taken from him, it might be relevant."

Brandon stared at her, incredulous. "Seriously? Why does it matter if something was stolen from him?"

Luiz, his gaze steady and thoughtful, interjected, "It's actually a good idea. If this is the work of a serial killer, recognizing patterns early on is crucial." He glanced pointedly at Edith and Brandon, his voice dropping to a low, ominous murmur. "Not that it matters much now, since I have a strong suspicion it's you two."

Brandon's fists tightened, his face reddening. "What did you say? I bet it's really you trying to tie up loose ends."

Luiz gave a nonchalant shrug, his broad shoulders rolling under the fabric of his shirt. "Accuse me all you want. I'll be coming for you once I have the evidence." With that, he turned on his heel and strode out of the room, not waiting for Brandon's response. Ava, driven by curiosity and urgency, followed Luiz.

The sight of Cedric's bloated body was jarring, and Ava forced herself not to focus too closely. She couldn't afford to let herself be overwhelmed by the grisly scene. Her gaze swept over the disarrayed oak table: wine glasses toppled, napkins and silverware scattered in a chaotic mess, and Cedric's vacant eyes staring up from his plate.

Ava kept her distance as Luiz approached Cedric's body, carefully searching his corpse. The others gathered around, and Ava felt a creeping sensation, as though the shadows in the room were beginning to slither along the walls. A shiver of unease washed over her, and she was on the verge of asking if anyone else felt the same when Luiz broke the silence.

"Does anyone know if Cedric carried a pocket watch? It seems the pocket where it should have been is empty."

Duncan answered in a subdued tone, "Yes, he did. I asked him for the time earlier, before dinner, and he pulled it out."

Luiz's brow furrowed. "Did he mention if it was of any particular significance to him?"

He replied, "He did. When I remarked on the design, he said it was a family heirloom from his father's side, or something like that."

A muscle in Luiz's jaw twitched. "I thought so. We should all head back to the living room."

Brandon's voice was a low growl. "I'm really getting sick of you ordering us around."

He ignored him, heading toward the living room with a purposeful stride. Ava exchanged glances with Jocelyn and Duncan, and they followed suit, as if guided by a shared instinct.

Edith and Brandon muttered to each other before trailing after the rest. Once in the living room, Ava plopped into an armchair near the fire. The clock above the mantle was shattered, its hands frozen at five o'clock, and she guessed it must be close to eight.

She longed to be back in her own home, curled up with Carter, watching a movie. She missed the warmth of his presence, the comfort of his heartbeat beneath her hand. Carter had been her anchor after the Wellingtons' suicide shattered her last shred of hope for Oliver. If his parents, who should have had more faith, had given up, how could she hold on?

Despite the support of her friends, grief, anger, and confusion had threatened to consume her. She had tried to numb the pain with alcohol and fleeting relationships, but nothing had eased the ache until she met Carter. His love and support had revived her, giving her a reason to keep going. Without him, she feared she might have followed Oliver's parents into despair.

Her reverie was interrupted as Duncan settled beside her on the couch, rubbing his slender hands toward the fire. Luiz took his place by the mantle, with Jocelyn sitting beside Duncan. Edith and Brandon positioned themselves at the other end of the fireplace, facing Ava.

Edith's voice was laced with mockery. "So, what's it going to be now, Luiz? More accusations?"

Luiz slipped his hands into his pockets and responded, "Not quite. I'd prefer to share my observations and reach a conclusion."

Brandon sneered, "And what's that?"

Luiz's shrug was casual, but his gaze was sharp. "Whether or not you two are responsible for the murders of Cedric Crawford and Audrey Ballard—and the entire scheme behind tonight's events."

15

Brandon's tawny eyes flared with fury as he growled, "You must be out of your mind! What evidence do you have to accuse us?"

Luiz scratched his jaw, his gaze thoughtful. "It's quite straightforward. There are six distinct explanations for tonight's events, and I intend to start with the least likely, working up to the most plausible, based on my observations." He let his eyes sweep over everyone in the room before he continued.

He raked a hand through his short, onyx hair, and the scar stretching from his temple to his nose seemed more pronounced in the flickering firelight. "First, consider that everyone here, except Ava, received an invitation threatening to reveal a personal secret if we didn't attend." Ava felt the weight of suspicious glances, but she tried to remain still. "Moreover, everyone here, besides Ava, was involved in Oliver's death."

Jocelyn shot up from her chair, her gaze icy and fierce. "I had nothing to do with his disappearance. I'm as clueless as Ava about what happened to him."

Shadows flickered over her delicate face as she fought to maintain her composure. Ava reached out, taking Jocelyn's slender hand, and guided her back into her seat.

"Hey," Ava said softly, "I know you didn't do anything. Don't listen to him." Jocelyn met her gaze with gratitude, nodding in response. Once Jocelyn was back on the couch, Ava turned sharply to Luiz, her voice dripping with fury. "Who the hell do you think you are? Jocelyn had nothing to do with Oliver's disappearance. She was his friend, for god's sake!"

Her indignation surged, flooding every inch of her being. "So, you think just because you're some highfalutin lawyer from Spain, you can waltz in here and accuse everyone of being murderers? You've creeped me out from the moment we met, with your whole silent bad-boy routine in the garden. Why aren't you the killer? You certainly seem like the type."

Luiz's eyes flared, simmering with a dangerous edge. "I'd be very careful about what you say next." The pure authority in his voice made her anger waver, but she met his gaze with as much defiance as she could muster. With a final glare, she dropped back into her chair, her rage still crackling in the air.

Luiz pinched the bridge of his nose and sighed deeply. "As I was saying, everyone here, except Ava, had some involvement with Oliver's death." He shot a pointed look at Jocelyn's defiant gaze, a muscle in his jaw twitching. "Although I can't pinpoint Jocelyn's exact role—my involvement was minimal—I have to assume she played some part."

He continued, "So, let's start with the least likely candidate for tonight's events: Duncan Dover." Duncan's eyes widened in surprise, but he wisely chose to remain quiet. "While Duncan would benefit from ensuring everyone stays quiet, he lacks both the means to unearth our personal secrets and the cunning required to orchestrate the events unfolding tonight."

Duncan bristled, "Are you saying I'm dumb?"

Edith's lips curled into a smirk. "Oh, poor Duncan. My sister didn't exactly have a special interest in you because of your intellect." Duncan's face reddened. Ava's curiosity piqued—was there some underlying history between Hazel, Oliver's mother, and Duncan?

Luiz dismissed Edith with a curt nod and addressed Duncan directly. "Not exactly. To orchestrate tonight's events would require a sharp, calculating mind, which you clearly lack. And frankly, I don't believe you have the disposition to commit murder."

Duncan started to speak, then hesitated, his words faltering.

Luiz moved on without skipping a beat. "The next unlikely suspect is Jocelyn. Even if she wasn't involved in Oliver's disappearance, the motive could be personal revenge. The murders tonight are ironically tied to the victims' sins. Jocelyn certainly has the means—wealth and influence—to uncover our secrets and orchestrate this chaos. But I doubt she's capable of murder, even if she might feel we deserve it."

Ava exhaled slowly, relief washing over her. Jocelyn's eyes, filled with gratitude, mirrored Ava's.

Luiz's muscles tensed as he folded his arms, his olive skin glowing from the firelight. "Now, I must consider myself. While I had both the opportunity and means to kill Cedric and Audrey tonight, I did not."

Edith erupted, "Really? That's your—"

Luiz raised a hand, his Spanish accent sharpening his tone. "Let me finish, and I will explain." Edith huffed and crossed her slender arms. Luiz continued, "The reason I am not at fault is simple: I have no motive. I was content with the way things were. As long as everyone kept their secrets, I had no reason to harm any of you."

Edith purred with a predatory gleam in her eye, "Oh, please. Don't fool yourself into thinking you wouldn't kill for the thrill. I know who you really are, Luiz. You're not just a lawyer—you—ki-"

Before she could finish, Luiz was suddenly in front of her. His hand clamped around her throat, lifting her with a single, powerful movement. Edith, her delicate features contorted in shock, clawed desperately at his hand. Her eyes were wide with fear as her attempts to scream were choked off.

Luiz's face was a mask of unbridled fury, his olive skin glowing in the firelight. His scar, a jagged line from temple to nose, shifted with every pulse of his rage. The shadows around them seemed to squirm and twist, as if relishing the violence erupting in the room.

With mere inches separating his face from hers, Luiz whispered, "You better shut your mouth, or I swear I'll kill you." Ava glanced at Brandon, who stood beside Edith, slack-jawed and unmoving. Fear gripped Ava as she wondered if there was about to be a third murder this dreadful night

Ava watched as Luiz released Edith, who collapsed to the floor, her blue dress spread beneath her. Edith rubbed her neck, red from Luiz's grip. Brandon quickly knelt beside her, one hand cradling her face, the other supporting her upper back.

Edith, her voice weak but filled with hatred, rasped, "I swear you'll pay for that." Luiz, unfazed, slipped his hands into his black trousers and calmly returned to his place, his face impassive.

He said with a nonchalant shrug, "As I was saying, I didn't kill Cedric and Audrey." From the corner of her eye, Ava saw Edith pushing herself to her feet, her eyes blazing as she glared at Luiz. "Now, moving on to the three more probable scenarios. The least likely of these is the worst-case scenario, which would be—"

Edith cut him off, her voice trembling with fury. "I'm done with your ridiculous theories. I won't stand here any longer, not after you nearly killed me. As far as I'm concerned, you're responsible for everything that's happened tonight." Without waiting for a response, Edith and Brandon stormed out of the living room, heading toward the staircase in the foyer.

Luiz raised a thin eyebrow. "Well, that seemed rather dramatic."

Ava lifted her chin defiantly and asked, "What was she about to say? What exactly do you do?"

Darkness clouded his brown eyes as he replied coldly, "That's none of your concern. Let's just hope you never find out." The threat in his voice sent a chill down her spine that even the firelight couldn't dispel.

Turning away, Ava focused on the photos lining the mantle. The framed photographs were noticeably less dusty than the rest of the house, suggesting they might have been placed there recently. She couldn't discern the details of the pictures from where she sat, but their haphazard arrangement struck her as suspicious. Distrustful of Luiz, Ava decided to wait until he left before examining them further.

Jocelyn broke the heavy silence, her voice tinged with curiosity. "What were you about to say before Edith interrupted?"

Luiz shrugged, his broad shoulders shifting with the motion, and sighed. "It's irrelevant now. I needed to observe their reactions to test the validity of my theory." His gaze shifted to Duncan with a probing look. "Actually, you might assist me with the explanation I was about to present."

Duncan's russet eyes widened, and he sat forward. "I can?"

Luiz nodded, his expression inscrutable. "Yes, you can. The possibility I was about to discuss is that Oliver himself might be orchestrating all of this. Are you absolutely certain he was dead when he was buried?"

Ava's heart pounded in her chest, and a sudden wave of dizziness made the room spin. She barely registered Duncan and Jocelyn's gasps of shock. The idea that Oliver, the boy she once knew, could be behind these monstrous acts was almost too much to bear. The thought of him being responsible made her stomach churn, leaving her on the brink of nausea.

Duncan drew a shaky breath. "I don't know," he admitted, his voice wavering. "I never went back to the burial site, but he looked dead when I buried him. There was so much blood... I don't see how he could have survived."

Ava's vision darkened with a mix of rage and disbelief, the room around her seeming to close in. Luiz's gaze remained cold and calculating as he continued, "Hmm, I doubt he could have survived too. The two most plausible explanations are that it's a close friend of Oliver seeking revenge or that it's Edith and Brandon tying up loose ends."

As Luiz spoke, he paced slowly across the room, his leather shoes scuffing against the carpet with each deliberate step. Ava watched, her knuckles white as she gripped the armrests of her chair, struggling to maintain her composure.

Luiz strode towards the foyer. "Be careful," he advised, his voice carrying across the room. "I'd stay away from Edith and Brandon."

The living room fell into a heavy silence as Luiz's footsteps faded. Ava took a deep breath, trying to calm her racing heart. She stood up and walked towards the mantle, her steps slow and deliberate against the plush carpet.

As she neared the mantle, she noticed the photographs had changed. The once-familiar wooden frames, now glinting with golden leaf accents, no longer held images of Oliver and his family. Instead, they were replaced by portraits of everyone currently in the house—each one captured in a crisp, unsettling detail.

Ava's breath hitched, and a high-pitched ringing filled her ears. Her heart pounded as she took in the array of photographs now gracing the mantle. Each frame, once an artifact of personal history, now felt like a chilling prophecy.

Cedric's photo showed him with his wife, a woman with a warm smile and soft eyes, and their two young boys, their faces full of innocence and joy. Beside it was Audrey, her usually stern expression softened as she held her daughter close, a tender moment captured in time.

Duncan was next, standing in a lush garden, his delicate frame and brown hair contrasting with the vibrant greenery around him.

Jocelyn's portrait was framed with her parents, her delicate features and elegant attire making her look like a porcelain doll amidst their protective presence.

Luiz's photo was of him with a diploma from a Spanish university. Brandon and Edith were pictured together on a sun-drenched beach, their tanned skin and carefree smiles betraying a moment of genuine relaxation.

Finally, there was Ava, beaming beside Oliver, their faces glowing with the kind of happiness that seemed too perfect to last.

Ava's breath hitched as she noticed the cracked glass in Cedric's and Audrey's frames. The realization struck her like a punch to the gut—the photos were arranged in the order of their deaths. Cedric and Audrey had been the first two victims, and the cracks in their frames were not random.

Her stomach lurched as she faced the implication: Duncan, framed in his serene garden setting, was next.

16

Ava turned to the others, her voice shaking as she said, "Hey, you guys might want to come take a look at this." Each word came out as a whisper from her parched throat.

Jocelyn, her golden hair catching the light as she tilted her head in curiosity, asked, "Why? What's going on?"

Ava continued, "It's photos of us. They're arranged in the order that we're going to be killed. Cedric's and Audrey's frames are cracked."

Duncan bolted upright, his face pale as he stumbled toward Ava. "No, no, no, I'm next. It's because of what we did to Oliver." The words ignited a spark in Ava's chest. She turned a hard glare toward him, her patience fraying. She knew Duncan would be easier to intimidate than Luiz.

"What the hell did you guys do to Oliver? I'm sick of being kept in the dark," Ava demanded.

Jocelyn, her expression taut with anxiety, added, "I'd like to know, too."

Duncan's gaze darted around the room. "Aren't you concerned about these photos? Shouldn't we go tell Luiz?"

Ava planted her hands firmly on her hips and declared, "Absolutely not. I don't trust him, especially after he threatened Edith." Her eyes flicked between Duncan and Jocelyn. "For now, you two are the only ones I trust not to be the killer."

Ava settled back into her armchair as Duncan plopped onto the couch, the picture of exhaustion. He met her gaze and let out a long sigh. "What I'm about to tell you, please don't share with Luiz or Edith. You were never meant to know."

She nodded, "I understand," and Jocelyn mirrored her gesture. Ava wouldn't confide in Edith; her intention was to go to the authorities as soon as she escaped this nightmare.

Duncan drew a deep breath. "What happened to Oliver was all Edith's idea. I wasn't involved in the plan. I didn't want any part of it, but I ended up seeing too much."

Ava's heart pounded heavily in her chest as she gently prodded, "What do you mean?"

His eyes welled with tears, his voice breaking as he confessed, "I was trimming the bushes on the east side of the house when I heard a commotion at the front. When I turned the corner, I saw Oliver lying motionless on the ground, blood pooling around his head. Edith, Brandon, and Audrey were standing over him, discussing their next move."

A deep sadness settled in Ava's stomach, threatening to overwhelm her. She wanted to scream at the injustice of it all but forced herself to stay calm as she asked, "How did they hurt him?"

Duncan replied, "Brandon had a baseball bat and used it to hit Oliver in the head. I think he swung a bit too hard. I rushed to help Oliver, but there was too much blood, and I couldn't stop the bleeding." He paused, wiping his eyes with the back of his hand.

He looked up, his face pale and haunted. "I asked them why they did it, and they told me everything."

Jocelyn placed a comforting hand on Duncan's shoulder and asked softly, "Why would they tell you and not just kill you?"

"They decided to change their plans and make me dig a grave for Oliver in the woods. Brandon threatened to kill me and my family if I said anything. I felt trapped, but now I see I had a choice, and I was a coward." His breath hitched as he looked down. "I dug a five-foot hole, and they just tossed him in there like trash."

Ava's vision narrowed as anger flooded her being. She was seconds away from storming upstairs and confronting Edith with lethal force. Duncan's gaze softened, and he said gently, "It wasn't your fault, Ava. Audrey drugged you with sleeping medication while you were drinking tea. There was nothing you could have done. None of this is your fault."

Relief crashed over Ava like a tidal wave, and the weight that had burdened her for years seemed to lift from her shoulders. Tears streamed down her cheeks as she buried her face in her hands and sobbed uncontrollably.

Jocelyn broke the silence. "So, they drugged Ava, hit Oliver in the head, and then buried him. Is that right?" Duncan nodded solemnly. "But why? What could have driven them to do this to Oliver?"

Duncan took a deep breath and explained, "From what I pieced together, Audrey despised Oliver. She often spoke to Edith and Brandon about how he tormented her. I don't know the details, but her hatred was deep. Edith and Brandon, on the other hand, were motivated by money."

Jocelyn tilted her head, curiosity etched across her face. "What do you mean?"

"Before Oliver was born, Edith was supposed to inherit the entire Wellington estate. Since Edward had no living relatives, or heir, the will stipulated that Edith, as Hazel's sister, would inherit everything. But when Oliver was born, they changed the will to name him as the successor."

Ava, her tears momentarily subsiding, asked, "What about Cedric? What was his role in all of this? Didn't the Wellingtons just revert the will to favor Edith after what happened to Oliver?"

Duncan shook his head. "No, the Wellingtons had changed their will before their deaths. They had decided to liquidate everything and donate the proceeds to charity. When Edith found out, she hired Cedric to alter the will and make her the beneficiary."

Ava furrowed her brow, deep in thought. "That explains why everyone else is here, but why were Jocelyn and I targeted?"

He slouched deeper into the couch. "Honestly, I don't know. Maybe they wanted to keep you alive to take the fall later? It seems to me that Edith or Luiz is behind all this. That's what makes the most sense."

Ava, though she now had the full story of Oliver's death, couldn't shake a nagging feeling. She turned to the others and asked, "Has anyone noticed anything odd about this house since we arrived?"

Jocelyn shook her head, her golden hair catching the dim light. "No, nothing unusual on my end. Duncan, have you noticed anything?"

"Nothing out of the ordinary," Duncan replied, his voice heavy with uncertainty. "Why? Did you see something strange?"

Ava felt a wave of self-doubt wash over her. "I don't know," she said, her voice trailing off. "It's just... this house feels alive. Like there's something malevolent lurking here. The shadows are darker than they should be, and it's almost like they're moving."

As if in response, the shadows on the walls seemed to stretch and wriggle, inching closer to her. The sinister presence she'd felt since her arrival seemed to hover at the edge of her consciousness, and she could almost hear faint, ghostly whispers threading through the air around her.

Duncan rubbed his chin, his expression thoughtful. "Maybe it's just the stress from everything that's happened tonight. This place is eerie, and you've been through a lot."

Ava let out a weak chuckle, shaking her head. "Yeah, maybe. It's probably just my mind playing tricks on me." She turned her gaze to the fire, focusing on the steady crackle and pop of the logs. The rhythmic sounds offered a semblance of normalcy, helping her to drown out the whispers that seemed to be trying to seduce her.

Duncan slowly stood up, but Ava's voice stopped him. "Wait, where are you going? It would be safer for us to stick together."

He looked back at her, a serene acceptance in his eyes. "I need to find out what the killer knows about me. And honestly, after what we did to Oliver, maybe we do deserve this."

Ava knew there was no convincing him otherwise, so she held her tongue. She glanced over at Jocelyn, who was lost in the mesmerizing dance of the fire, her face thoughtful and distant. With a resigned sigh, Duncan walked out of the living room and into the foyer.

From the corner of her eye, Ava thought she saw—or perhaps heard—the glass in Duncan's picture frame crack.

17

The crackling of the fire was the only sound that broke the silence in the spacious living room. Ava rose from her seat and settled onto the velvety couch beside Jocelyn. The dim light cast soft shadows across Jocelyn's delicate, heart-shaped face, highlighting her golden hair that seemed to glow even in the low light. Ava couldn't help but wonder what kind of twisted individual would target someone like Jocelyn.

What dark secret lay beneath her innocent exterior?

Jocelyn turned to face Ava. "Hey, can I ask you something?"

"Sure, ask me anything," Ava said.

Jocelyn's eyes, still wide, searched Ava's face. "How have you stayed so calm tonight? I've been terrified ever since walking through the front door."

Ava considered the question for a moment, then sighed. "Well, I'd like to say it's because I'm a strong and confident woman," she said, flexing her muscles with a wry chuckle. "But, to be honest, I've barely been holding it together. The last seven years have been a mess. When you're constantly battling depression and drowning in guilt, it's hard to feel much worse."

She gave a small, understanding smile. "I see. I'm still trying to process what really happened to Oliver, and I don't know who to trust."

Ava gently placed a hand on hers. "I know how you feel. For years, I have wanted to know what happened to him. I just hope he didn't suffer. Also, you can trust me. I promise I'm not the one behind all of this"

She nodded, but her lips remained sealed.

"There's something I'd like to ask you," Ava said, her gaze steady. Jocelyn gave a slight nod, a silent signal to continue.

Ava leaned in slightly. "If you don't mind me asking, what is your secret? What are you risking your life to protect?"

Jocelyn's face fell into a shadow of despair. She sighed heavily. "The secret I'm protecting is that I'm in love."

Ava frowned, her confusion evident. "What do you mean?"

Jocelyn looked away, her eyes distant. "Before Oliver disappeared, I was seeing our stable boy in secret. We planned to run away together once I was of age to marry. While my parents intended for me to marry Oliver, I used him as a distraction while I was actually being courted by someone else."

Ava's eyes widened in surprise. She hadn't expected someone so young and seemingly innocent to harbor such a scandalous secret. Her curiosity piqued, she asked, "Does he make you happy?"

Jocelyn's face lit up with a soft, genuine smile. "He makes me the happiest woman on the planet. I don't care if running away with him would ruin my family's reputation. He's worth more to me than all the money and influence in the world."

Ava rested her chin on her hand, a thoughtful expression crossing her face. "I know exactly what you mean. I have someone like that too."

Jocelyn's eyes brightened with interest. "Oh, really? What's his name?"

"His name is Carter," Ava said, her voice softening with affection. "He's my fiancé now. He proposed to me recently." Ava held out her hand, showing Jocelyn the diamond ring glinting in the firelight. "He's the best boyfriend—and now the best fiancé—in the world. He helped me through one of the darkest periods of my life."

Jocelyn's gaze lingered on the sparkling diamond, her smile widening. "That's wonderful. How did you two meet?"

Ava looked past Jocelyn and lost herself in memory. She breathed, "It was two years ago when we met, and he changed my life."

✳ ✳ ✳ ✳ ✳ ✳ ✳ ✳ ✳ ✳ ✳ ✳ ✳ ✳

The coffee cup in Ava's hands trembled as she struggled to keep her composure. The sting of pain from the heat of the cup was the only thing tethering her to reality. The noise of the bustling coffee shop turned into a droning sound that filled her head. The smell of coffee, which she usually found pleasant, now caused her stomach to roil like a violent sea.

She distantly heard someone speaking to her, but paid them no mind. It wasn't until that person gently laid a hand on her shoulder that she looked up. The sight of the gorgeous man before her cleared some of the fog in her brain.

"Excuse me, miss. Are you okay?" His voice was smooth and concerned, cutting through the haze of Ava's thoughts. He had a ruggedly handsome face, with striking green eyes and black, wavy hair swept to the side. Ava found herself mesmerized by him, as though she could stare at him all day.

She hadn't realized she'd been crying until now. She must have looked like an idiot.

Wiping her eyes with the back of her hand, Ava managed softly, "Yeah, I'm okay."

The man's brow furrowed, but a wry smile touched his lips. "Right. Because anyone who's crying alone in a coffee shop is definitely doing just fine."

She rolled her eyes and scoffed. "You know, if you're trying to help me feel better, you're not doing a great job." Despite herself, a smile tugged at the corners of her mouth.

He grinned, his eyes twinkling with mischief. "I'd say I'm doing a pretty good job since you've stopped crying." He paused, his gaze lingering on her face. Leaning in slightly, he asked gently, "Is it okay if I ask what upset you? I'm Carter, by the way."

He extended a hand, and after a brief hesitation, Ava reached across the table and took it. His rough, calloused hand felt solid against her smooth, delicate skin. "I'm Ava. Nice to meet you. You can sit down if you'd like."

Carter's hand was warm and reassuring. He was undeniably beautiful, and she couldn't seem to look away.

She took a trembling breath and, after he settled into his seat, said, "I just learned that someone I cared about was declared dead after being missing for the past five years. And his parents…" Tears began to well up in her eyes, but Carter gently placed his hand on top of hers.

"It's okay if you can't bring yourself to talk about it," he said softly.

Ava sniffled and glanced at their hands, which seemed to fit together like puzzle pieces. "No, it's okay. I have to face this eventually." She inhaled deeply, gathering her composure. "The parents of the boy I was an au pair for… they killed themselves. The mother overdosed on sleeping medications, and the father… he shot himself in his study."

Carter's brows furrowed in concern. "I'm really sorry to hear that."

* * * * * * * * * * * * *

"And before I knew it, an hour had passed, and we went on a walk where he asked me out. We've been together ever since." Every time Ava thought back to that moment with Carter, she couldn't stop the smile that would spread across her face.

Jocelyn nodded, a warm smile lighting up her face. "It's a beautiful story, and I can see how much you love him." Her smile slowly faded, and a hint of sadness crept into her eyes. "I wish I had the same freedom to love openly as you do." Ava's heart ached for her, and she struggled to find the right words.

They sat in companionable silence for a few moments. Ava finally said, "I hope you find a way to live the life you want with the one you love. He's a lucky man."

Jocelyn's smile returned as she stood, smoothing out the wrinkles in her dress. "Thank you. And I'm a lucky woman, too. He's truly wonderful."

She began to move toward the foyer, but Ava called out, "Wait, where are you going? It's not safe to be alone."

"Earlier, Charles said that evidence of our secrets are hidden within this house, remember? I need to find mine. You know, you're welcome to come with me if you'd like."

Ava tilted her head, mulling it over. She chuckled softly and replied, "Well, that certainly beats staying here alone."

The Killer

18

The urge to kill again has been overwhelming since I killed that boorish woman, Audrey. Oh, how I had fun chopping her up. These fools are so easy to play with since they don't suspect me. I must keep it like this for as long as possible.

I stalked toward the room at the end of the dimly lit hallway, dust stirring with each step. The hallway was lined with faded wallpaper, its floral patterns peeling away to reveal the bare, cracked plaster beneath. Photos of an idyllic family hung crookedly on the walls, their frames dusty and neglected. A family that is dead, forgotten by the world.

The air was heavy with silence, broken only by the faint voices seeping from the room to my left, most likely Brandon and Edith. Ava and Jocelyn were still downstairs, their laughter faint and distant. I continued down the hallway toward my target, the shadows stretching and curling like serpents waiting to strike.

I crept toward the cracked door, and inside, I heard him rummaging and muttering to himself. I carefully pushed open the door and slipped into the bedroom.

The room, once belonging to Edward and Hazel Wellington, had remained untouched since their deaths. The king-sized bed dominated the space, its ornate, carved headboard and footboard draped in white, plush linens and an array of decorative pillows.

Elegant but now dust-covered furniture was scattered around the room. An antique vanity with a tarnished silver mirror stood against one wall, its surface cluttered with old, forgotten trinkets. A chaise lounge, its once-velvety upholstery faded and worn, rested near the window, which was shrouded in heavy, dusty drapes.

The room was enveloped in darkness, with only the faint moonlight filtering through the cracks in the heavy curtains to provide any illumination. The moon's pale light cast long, ghostly shadows. The air was laden with the musty scent of disuse, mingling with the faint aroma of old wood and fabric.

My focus was on the person frantically rummaging through the nightstand on the right side of the bed. My blood thrummed as I slowly slinked across the room, my footsteps silenced by the plush rug covering the floor. The voices howled in my ear and the adrenaline rush that I craved started to flow through me.

I loomed over my prey, my shadow stretching out like a dark specter. It crept around me and slithered over his shoulders, curling and tightening. He froze, terror gripping him as he stared at the creeping shadows. When his gaze met mine, his face drained of color, turning a sickly green.

He turned slowly, his mouth working like a fish out of water, but no words emerged. I purred, "Oh, how I've been looking forward to this."

His face went a shade paler, eyes wide with panic. "Y-y-you're b-behind t-t-this? I'm s-so sorry."

A shadow traced a gentle path across his face. I tilted my head, a chuckle slipping from my lips. "Of course, it's me. Who else could it be? Any last words?"

He seemed to find a strange calm, accepting his fate with a resigned air. Meeting my gaze, he said, "I was a coward that day. I deserve this."

A shadow slithered up his face and coiled around his throat. His eyes widened in horror as he clawed desperately at his neck. He tried to scream, but the dense mass of shadows choking him stifled any sound.

I crooned, a cruel smile curving my lips. "Don't worry. This isn't what's going to kill you. I just don't want you making any noise while I work."

19

Ava and Jocelyn meandered through the library's labyrinthine stacks, which had taken on the air of a mausoleum as the night deepened. The sconces, a recent addition revealed by their relative lack of dust, threw an unsettling glow across the room. The flickering candlelight barely penetrated the narrow walkways between the bookcases, leaving deep pockets of darkness.

Ava broke the silence with a question, "So, what exactly are you looking for?"

Jocelyn's voice floated around the corner, "I'm searching for love letters between me and Daniel, my beloved. I'm also hoping to find any photographs this stalker might have taken of us."

Ava responded with a thoughtful hum, "Maybe there's a 'creepy stalker' section hidden somewhere in these stacks."

Jocelyn chuckled, "May—" but her laughter was abruptly cut off by an unearthly, shrieking wail that echoed through the house. They exchanged a brief glance before rushing out of the library and climbing up the stairs.

Beyond their footsteps, the house was unnervingly quiet, as if the shriek had silenced everything that breathed. They climbed the two levels of creaking wooden stairs until they reached the second-floor landing. Edith and Brandon burst from a room down the hall to their left, and Luiz came barreling up the stairs.

Edith fumbled with her disheveled hair, while Brandon hastily tucked his white dress shirt into his trousers. Whipping her head towards Ava, Edith demanded, "Did anyone else hear that ungodly shriek?"

Ava nodded, "Yeah, that's why we came running up here." She began to look around with rising panic. "Where's Duncan?" They all turned toward the room at the end of the hall, where a faint flicker of candlelight danced beneath the door.

Luiz stepped around Ava and Jocelyn, heading straight for the room. "I'll check it out," he grumbled. "You guys stay here." He moved down the hall, but Brandon stepped into his path.

"How about I go with you? Just in case someone's waiting in there."

Luiz shot him a disdainful look. "Do what you want, but if you pull any stunts, I'll kill you." He didn't wait for a response, pushing on toward the room.

The others held their breath as Luiz and Brandon approached. The thick rug underfoot muffled their steps. They inched the door open, entering with their fists clenched, prepared for whatever might await them.

After a few agonizing moments, Luiz let out a sharp curse, and Brandon stumbled out of the room, his angular face drained of color, green with the shock of whatever he had seen.

Ava asked, "What was it? What's in there?"

Brandon looked as if he might be sick, his hand running shakily through his messy hair. "It's Duncan," he managed to choke out, but he couldn't say more.

Edith was already at his side, wrapping him in her arms, whispering soothingly.

Ava's face was ashen with shock as she glanced at Jocelyn. She leaned in, her voice barely a whisper, "Come on, let's go take a look." She took Jocelyn's hand, and Jocelyn nodded silently.

As they approached the room, Ava's thoughts drifted to Carter. She remembered their countless moments together: the long walks in the park where she'd shared secrets she'd never told anyone else, the ice cream dates, and their adventures in far-off places.

Ava's heart clenched with a desperate hope—she needed to make it through the night to see him again, to begin their life together.

As they entered the room, the sharp, metallic scent of iron hit Ava like a wall. Jocelyn let out a piercing scream and pressed herself against Ava. The sight before them threatened to bring her to her knees.

Duncan lay on the bed with his arms and legs spread open. Blood streaked across the walls and drenched the bed, the deep crimson a stark contrast from the dusty, white comforter. His throat bore a deep gash with blood that still trickled from it. His body was riddled with deep stab wounds, and flecks of gore spilled out from the slashes.

Ava thought she was going to faint at the sight of the pool of blood that concentrated at his crotch, which appears to have been lacerated. A crimson knife protruded from Duncan's mouth, his face twisted in terror. She turned her gaze to Luiz, who stood on the far side of the bed.

Luiz's face was flushed red, twisted with raw rage. With a roar, he grabbed the dead lamp from the nightstand and hurled it against the opposite wall. The loud crash made Ava and Jocelyn jump, and Edith and Brandon rushed into the room.

Edith's eyes stood out vividly against her ghostly white face as she took in the sight of Duncan. Ava feared she might faint. Edith leaned on Brandon, who shouted at Luiz, "What the hell happened?"

His gaze turned predatory as he snarled, "I'm done with this. I don't like being played with." His eyes fixed on Ava. "Is anything missing from Duncan?"

She took a sharp breath and said, "If you think I'm going to touch his body, you're out of your mind." Luiz narrowed his eyes and sighed, then moved to the body and checked the pockets of Duncan's jacket. Finding nothing, he turned Duncan over to search his pants.

After flipping him back, Luiz wiped his bloodied hands on his black suit. "There's nothing on him, so maybe the killer took his wallet."

Edith appeared to regain her composure, though Ava noticed the tear stains on her cheeks and how her curly hair clung to her damp face. She asked, "Why would someone want his wallet?"

Ava suggested, "Maybe it had photos of his family or a cherished memento."

Jocelyn added in a shaky voice, "His wallet was one of his most prized possessions."

Edith shot her a scornful look. "And how would you know that?"

Jocelyn's gaze grew distant, as if she were recalling a far-off memory. "When I used to visit Oliver, Duncan would show me the photos in his wallet. He said his parents died when he was young and that those photos were all he had left of them. The only family he had left was his younger brother."

Edith's expression faltered, and Luiz frowned in frustrated thought. The room fell into a heavy silence, and just as Ava was about to speak, something caught her eye. The drawer of the nightstand on the right side of the bed was slightly open.

Ava moved towards the blood-splattered nightstand and began sifting through the contents. She discovered Hazel's diary, a simple brown leather journal, and quickly slid it out, hoping it might hold some crucial information. Among the other items, she found old letters that made her breath catch in her throat.

They were love letters between Hazel Wellington, Oliver's mother, and Duncan. Ava's hand flew to her mouth as she read through the steamy, intimate notes. She turned to the group, one hand keeping the journal hidden behind her, her voice steady yet filled with revelation. "I just found these love letters between Hazel and Duncan. They were having an affair."

Jocelyn gasped, her hands flying to her mouth, while Luiz merely raised an eyebrow. Edith and Brandon, however, seemed unfazed.

Ava's gaze snapped to Edith, fury in her voice. "Did you know about this?"

Edith averted her eyes from Duncan, her tone dripping with indifference. "Well, duh. Who do you think my sister talked to about it?"

Luiz stepped forward, his hands clenched into fists. "You didn't think to mention this?" As he spoke, the shadows in the room seemed to writhe and slither across the walls.

Edith glanced at Brandon, who looked pale and vacant, and scoffed. "Who cares? It's not the first time one of the Wellingtons cheated." She flicked her gaze to Ava and Jocelyn. "If you're so concerned about me keeping secrets, I could always share what I know about you."

Luiz's tawny eyes flashed with menace. "I wouldn't do that. It's none of their business."

Edith's smirk was one of triumph. "Then stop hounding me about what I choose to share."

A hush swept through the room once more. The new revelations fought for space with the confusion swirling through Ava's mind as she struggled to put the pieces of this macabre puzzle together.

Ava suddenly recalled the photographs from downstairs. "There was a line of photos of all of us on the mantle downstairs. Cedric's and Audrey's were already broken."

Edith raised an eyebrow. "So what? Why does that matter, aside from being creepy?"

Ava took a shaky breath. "I think they were arranged in the order of our deaths. And Duncan was next."

Luiz's eyes narrowed. "Who's after Duncan?"

"It's me."

20

Luiz removed his black suit jacket, folding it over his arm. Deep lines had etched themselves under his eyes, like canyons forming above his cheekbones. He looked thoroughly exhausted.

He wiped his face with his free hand and said, "Can you show me these photos?" Ava nodded and left the room, with Jocelyn right behind her.

As they walked down the hall, Ava's gaze took in the tattered photos hanging askew on the peeling walls. Family portraits of Oliver and his relatives hung limply, swaying slightly as if stirred by a ghostly breeze.

After discovering how Oliver had treated Audrey and Jocelyn, Ava struggled to reconcile the image of the sweet little boy in the photographs with the man he had become. How had she missed it? Had he merely pretended to be kind? Did he ever truly care for her?

Lost in these thoughts, she found herself back in the living room. Her eyes widened in shock as she scanned the mantle.

All the photos were gone.

She turned to Luiz, her voice shaking. "I swear the photos were right here." She spun to Jocelyn, her desperation evident. "Tell him. Tell him they were here."

Jocelyn nodded. "It's true. All the photos were right there on the mantle. Whoever did this must have taken them."

Ava sank into the armchair, fatigue weighing heavily on her. Jocelyn took a seat on the sofa beside her, fear etched into her delicate features.

Edith and Brandon positioned themselves on the left side of the mantle, Brandon's expression stony and unreadable. Edith said, "Maybe it would help to figure out where everyone was while Duncan was being killed. Brandon and I were upstairs in one of the other rooms." Her gaze flicked toward Ava and Jocelyn with clear disdain.

Ava fidgeted in her seat, spinning her ring. "Jocelyn and I were in the library."

Edith's smirk grew. "So that just leaves you, Luiz." Her eyes slid to him like a cat sizing up its prey.

He snapped back, "I was downstairs, just so you know. It couldn't have been me."

Edith's gaze remained unyielding. "Not entirely true. You could have killed Duncan and then come back downstairs."

Luiz rolled up his sleeves and tossed his jacket onto the other armchair. "Ava and Jocelyn were down here too. They would have seen me if I had gone up the stairs from the living room."

Ava shot back, "We were actually in the library together the entire time." Her mind raced with possibilities.

Luiz could have snatched the photos before heading upstairs to kill Duncan. It was entirely possible that Luiz was the culprit, but what about his earlier outburst? Could it have been an act

Could Edith and Brandon be involved? Were they playing a role too? Or was someone else framing them? Ava's head pounded with frustration and the rising tide of helplessness.

The living room seemed to close in on her, the flickering light from the dimly lit fireplace casting uneasy shadows on the walls.

Luiz's face turned pale, and Edith's sneer deepened. "Well, it looks like we've finally figured out who's behind all of this."

His expression twisted with rage as he bared his teeth. "I have nothing to do with this! If anyone's responsible for tonight's carnage, it's you two."

Edith raised a manicured hand and chuckled, "Oh, darling. The game is over. I must admit, you had me fooled for a while. I almost believed someone else might be behind this."

Luiz raked his fingers through his hair in frustration. "That doesn't make any sense! What about that inhuman shriek? I would have been caught by Ava and Jocelyn as they were coming out of the library to investigate." His argument sparked a flicker of doubt in Ava's mind.

Edith merely sighed, "Maybe you were just really quick. I don't care. It's you, end of story." She glanced at Brandon, seeking validation, but his face remained impassive and vacant, as if his mind were miles away.

Edith clicked her tongue and shook her head. Ava, eager to shift the focus, asked, "Are we sure all the doors and windows are locked?"

Luiz interjected, "I'm fairly certain that if the windows aren't boarded up, they're at least chained together."

Edith retorted, "So why not just break them open?"

"Because the butlers are still out there, armed with guns. You wouldn't make it past the property line."

Edith crossed her arms and sneered, "We're just supposed to take your word for it? For all we know, you could be lying."

Luiz rolled his eyes in exasperation. "If you don't want to believe me, fine. But that doesn't change the fact that we're trapped here. Whoever is behind this is clearly a genius."

21

The crackling fire filled the silence that followed, casting eerie, dancing shadows across Edith's, Brandon's, and Luiz's faces—a vivid battle of light and darkness playing out on their features.

Edith fixed Luiz with a sharp look and asked, "How so?"

He sighed deeply. "The mastermind behind this night has crafted a situation where we're set up to lose. If we run, we die. If we panic, we'll end up killing each other. If we do nothing, we still die. And if we manage to survive, our secrets will be exposed and our lives destroyed."

Ava breathed, "So, what should we do?"

A flicker of dismay crossed Luiz's face. "I don't think there's anything to do. Tonight has been about revenge. It was over for us the moment we set foot in this house; we just didn't know it."

Edith interrupted sharply, "But that's only true if someone else is behind all of this. It's simply not possible!"

Luiz slammed his hand onto the mantle with a resounding thud and thundered, "And why not? Why is it so hard to believe that it's not one of us?" His gaze locked onto Ava, desperation evident in his eyes. "Did Oliver have any friends from school or other families? Anyone who might have cared if he went missing?"

Ava tilted her head, thinking for a moment. "I'm honestly not sure. Oliver didn't talk much about school or who he was close to. He never really had anyone over when I was his au pair."

Edith threw up her hands in exasperation. "See? It has to be one of us because Oliver had no close connections when he was alive."

The shadows in the room twisted and writhed on the walls, as if mocking the group. The presence that had lurked at the edge of Ava's consciousness seemed to revel in her confusion. If she focused hard enough, she could almost hear whispers drifting through the house—hypnotic, insidious murmurs that threatened to pull her under their influence. Were the others hearing these voices too?

Jocelyn's terrified scream yanked Ava back to reality. She gripped her head with both hands as tears streamed down her cheeks and splattered onto the sofa.

"No, no, no! I can't do this anymore!" Jocelyn cried, her eyes darting wildly around the room. Panic consumed her features. "We're all going to die! Can't you hear them? They're saying he's going to kill us, and there's nothing we can do to stop it!"

Before anyone could react, Jocelyn sprang from the couch and dashed out of the room, the flickering firelight casting erratic shadows as she raced past.

Ava stared, stunned by the complete breakdown she had just witnessed. She was surprised Jocelyn had held it together this long, but what did she mean about the voices? Were they real? Was Jocelyn hearing them too?

Her gaze shifted to Brandon's vacant, distant expression. Was he hearing them as well? Theories churned in her mind.

She needed to read Hazel's diary.

Edith chuckled darkly. "Well, that was quite dramatic." She fixed Luiz with a piercing look, like a serpent poised to strike. "I wonder who the 'he' she was referring to might be?"

Luiz's jaw tightened. He growled, "I don't know. I'd like to figure that out just as much as you."

Edith rolled her eyes and sighed. "Very well. Keep playing your little game if you wish. But if you come after us, you'll die trying." She tugged Brandon's limp form toward the foyer.

With them gone, Ava and Luiz were left alone in the dim, stuffy living room. Leaning against the brick mantle, he exhaled, "Don't worry. I'm not going to kill you."

Ava relaxed further into the comfortable chair and let out a breath. "Funny, I was going to say the same thing to you."

A corner of Luiz's thin mouth twitched upward. "Who do you think is behind this? Edith and Brandon, or someone else?"

"I honestly don't know. This whole situation is so twisted and convoluted."

He chuckled, a dry, humorless sound. "You've got that right."

Ava hesitated before inquiring, "Can I ask you something?"

"Go ahead."

"What's your connection to the Wellingtons? I know you had something to do with Oliver's death, but why?"

His eyes widened with surprise, but he took a deep breath and closed them. "I never intended to tell you, but if I'm going to die, I might as well make my confession." Luiz pulled a simple, worn rosemary sprig from his jacket pocket and pressed a kiss to it.

Ava asked softly, "Are you Catholic?"

Luiz chuckled quietly. "Not really. This belonged to my mother. I never went to Mass with her much, nor did I care for the Catholic Church." His eyes shimmered with unshed tears, which he wiped away with the back of his hand.

Ava pressed gently, "What happened to your mother?"

"She died almost ten years ago. The doctor said it was from illness, but I believe it was from heartbreak." Ava tilted her head in confusion but kept silent. "Before I was born, my mother fell in love with an Englishman. His name was Edward Wellington. He swept her off her feet." His voice flickered in anger at the mention of Oliver's father.

He continued, "When I was a teenager, he'd visit us occasionally, even after he married Hazel. He'd promise to bring me to England and make me his heir." His hands clenched into fists, eyes narrowing with intensity. "But then Oliver was born, and he cast us aside. He stopped visiting, cut off all contact."

Veins bulged on the back of his hands as his anger flared. "My mother never lost hope that he'd return for us. But after she fell ill and died, I was left alone—no mother, no father."

A tear traced down Ava's cheek as she murmured, "That's terrible. I'm so sorry that happened to you."

Luiz nodded, taking a deep breath. "When I learned about Oliver, I vowed revenge against Edward. That's how I got involved with Edith. I helped Edith plan everything. With my...expertise, I gave her advice on how to talk to the police after the disappearance and how to commit the crime without leaving physical evidence."

Ava asked, "And what about your secret? What are you trying to protect?"

He scratched his neck, his gaze distant. "The truth is, I'm one of the biggest drug lords in Barcelona, Spain. Despite my public role as a lawyer, I've only ever prosecuted my rivals. I've never cared about the city's welfare—just money and power." He fixed her with a hard stare that pinned her in place. "I've killed. I've tortured. I've done unspeakable things for material gain." His eyes grew distant. "It seems karma is finally catching up with me."

Chills rippled through Ava's frame as she recalled their encounters—his immediate, disconcerting aura of intimidation, his unnervingly calm demeanor around the dead, his effortless threats against Edith.

She gazed at the fire, trying to process the enormity of his confession. Finally, she dared to meet his eyes and stated, "I don't really know what to say, but thank you for sharing. "

A fleeting sense of relief crossed his face, only to vanish just as quickly.

He nodded, smoothing his crumpled white shirt. "I'm going to search the house and find the leech behind this. I doubt it's Edith and Brandon, but stay wary of them." His gaze roamed the room, scrutinizing every shadow and crevice. "I've felt watched since I arrived at this creepy place. If someone's lurking, I'll find them."

He headed for the foyer, but Ava called after him, "Be careful, Luiz. There's been enough death tonight." He nodded and departed, leaving her alone in the quiet room, with only the dying fire for company.

Finally by herself, Ava retrieved Hazel's diary. The worn, brown leather journal had her name delicately engraved in shimmering gold on the cover. Ava hoped this journal held the answers she desperately sought. She cracked open the small book and flipped to the last entry, thinking it would be more efficient to start at the end.

As she reached the final entry, she nearly collapsed when she saw the date—it was the same day of Hazel's suicide. Her breath hitched as she read the final words of Hazel Wellington.

$$* * * * * * * * * * * * * *$$

It has been five years since Oliver disappeared. I fear that I shall never see him again. My husband has grown distant, as though a sea separates us, and no longer shares my bed.

Where did it all go wrong?

I have often looked back at my life to find the answer to this question, and it seems I always come back to the same place: this cursed house.

Oh, how I miss the days before we moved into this place. My darling Edward used to be such a kind and devoted man before inheriting this estate. How he used to laugh, buy me flowers, and compliment me before we lived here.

But those days stopped long ago.

A couple of years after we moved into the manor, he started to become cold and inattentive. He began taking business trips every other week, as if he couldn't wait to be rid of me. While I might want to blame him, I must admit that I was no better. I directed my passions toward other men and turned to the bottle to drown my sorrow.

I had hoped that having a child would bring us back to our former selves—a loving, caring, and devoted couple who cared only for each other.

But that never happened.

I pity our son for having us as parents. As I reach the end of my wretched existence, which ends tonight, I can see clearly once again.

I write now to whoever finds this, hoping that it will be discovered so the truth can be revealed. The truth about this house and Oliver. I must admit that I was somewhat untruthful about Oliver in the beginning because I have finally learned the truth about his disappearance.

I know it because he told me.

Except, it wasn't the Oliver I remember. This Oliver was angry, hateful, and full of wrath. Gone was the sweet and kind young man that I knew—or so I thought. Now, I have suspicions that he has always been this way.

A monster that hid its true form from its parents.

I learned how my despicable sister and the staff organized the scheme to get rid of Oliver. Oh, how blind I was to the danger surrounding him! Even though he was a monster, am I wrong to still love him? My own flesh and blood?

I admit I am conflicted in my soul. I could see the darkness swirling in Oliver, yet I still loved him. Maybe that makes me a monster too, for I failed him as a mother. I was never there to nurture him and teach him right from wrong.

Even though I want to blame myself, I know that there is another responsible party. There is something evil in this house that has corrupted our family. It brought out the worst in us. It seduced us, and we lost ourselves to the sweet promises it offered.

I warn whoever is reading this to never return to the manor. It is a place where you will lose yourself if you stay too long.

It is our fault. If we hadn't lived here when Oliver was born, perhaps he would have grown up to be a normal boy. Perhaps he wouldn't be the creature he is today.

There is one more thing I must write to ease my conscience. Ava, if you are reading this, I'm so sorry for blaming you for his disappearance. I know now that it was not your fault. I'm sorry that Edward and I abandoned you, someone who was like family, so long ago.

I hope that you can forgive us. And I hope that we can be forgiven after this life.

✳ ✳ ✳ ✳ ✳ ✳ ✳ ✳ ✳ ✳ ✳ ✳ ✳ ✳

Tears streamed down Ava's face as she finished reading the diary, the broken fragments inside her slowly mending. The implications of Hazel's words swirled in her mind, but new questions surfaced.

Why hadn't she noticed the malevolent presence while she was an au pair? Why was it only now revealing itself? Where had this evil force come from, and how could she possibly banish it from the house?

A sudden, sobering thought struck Ava, almost knocking the breath from her lungs.

Oliver was still alive.

She bolted from her chair, her heart pounding as she turned towards the foyer. The photographs on the mantle flashed in her mind—each one now laden with grim significance. Panic tightened in her chest as she dashed to the foyer from the living room.

She had to find Jocelyn. She had to warn everyone. Oliver was still out there, and they needed to know.

The Killer

22

I eased the heavy wooden door of the library open. The whispers of the shadows told me Jocelyn was inside and that Ava had discovered my mother's journal.

Fortunately, the others were still gathered in the living room, leaving me a small window of opportunity. The door groaned softly as it swung wide, the musty scent of mothballs filling the air.

I slipped into the dimly lit library, my pulse quickening with anticipation. The room was shrouded in darkness, save for the glow of the candles casting eerie shadows on the walls. My plan was simple: end Jocelyn's life swiftly and silently. I had waited too long for this moment.

Oh, how I've been waiting for this day.

I stepped into the heart of the library, navigating past the rows of neglected bookshelves. My ears were tuned to the faint, pitiful whimpering emanating from the far corner of the room. Each step I took on the creaky hardwood floor felt like a drumbeat in the stillness.

Normally, I'd have moved with more stealth, but tonight was different. Tonight, the game was reaching its climax.

My mouth watered with anticipation as I drew closer. Nothing and no one would stand in my way. Tonight, revenge was within reach, and my enemies would pay.

I rounded the corner at the end of the pathway, and there she was—Jocelyn, curled up and trembling in the dim light. Her head snapped up at the sound of my footsteps halting.

"Who's there?" she whispered, her voice quivering in the shadows. The light from the sconces barely touched this corner, leaving her straining to see through the darkness.

I crooned, "Well, well, Jocelyn. It's been a while, hasn't it?" Her eyes widened with pure dread.

"No... It can't be. You're supposed to be dead."

I folded my arms and drawled, "What can I say? I'm hard to kill." I took a few deliberate steps closer, savoring her fear. "You know, I was quite distraught when I found out you were cheating on me back in the day."

Her voice broke as she cried, "I'm sorry, Oliver. I never loved you. We might have been forced together by our families, but my heart... it belonged to someone else."

White-hot rage surged through me, and I hurled books from the shelves, sending them crashing to the floor. "I loved you!" I roared, my voice laced with fury. "What did the stable boy have that I didn't?"

"He had a heart, Oliver," she gasped, her voice shaking. "And goodness. You only had darkness in your core."

I prowled closer, looming over her. "You belonged to me!" I snarled. "If you had stayed loyal and not sullied yourself with another man, maybe you wouldn't be in this position."

I crouched down, forcing myself into her terrified gaze. Her small frame quivered under my intense scrutiny, and I could almost taste the fear emanating from her. My body yearned to end her, but I fought to control the urge.

I leaned in close, my voice a whisper. "You know, once I've finished with everyone here, I think I'll go after your boyfriend next." Her eyes widened in horror, and a small gasp escaped her lips. "That way, instead of just one fleeting life together, you'll have all of eternity to be together."

Her pleas broke through the silence, tears streaming down her face. "No, please, don't hurt him! I'll do anything. Just please, don't hurt him."

I grinned cruelly. "You crushed my heart when I found out about your betrayal." I slid a long, wicked knife from a sheath on my waist and wiggled it in front of her face.

I hissed gleefully, "I think I'll carve out yours."

23

Ava burst through the wooden double doors to the library and fell to the ground. Sobs wracked her body as she beheld Jocelyn's lifeless body in the center of the dusty, aged room.

Ava crawled to the corpse, but she couldn't see through the blurriness of her tears. When she wiped her eyes, Ava thought she was going to vomit. Jocelyn's face was ashen and twisted in a frozen moment of terror, with blood flecked across her facial features.

Letters were strewn across her body, and her heart was speared to the floor by a knife. Blood pooled underneath the organ, and she tried not to look at the gaping hole in her chest.

Ava knelt beside her friend, her silent sobs echoing in the quiet, dusty library. The weight of grief and helplessness pressed down on her like a relentless storm. To see someone so vibrant and full of life—someone she had cared for—ripped away so cruelly was almost unbearable.

Through her tears, Ava noticed scattered pages clinging to Jocelyn's body. Her trembling hand reached for one, revealing it to be a love letter. They were from Jocelyn to her fiancé, Thomas. Each page she read ignited a burning anger within her, transforming her despair into a searing rage. The more she uncovered their love story, the flame of anger inside her grew into a raging wildfire.

Ava's grief turned into a fierce resolve. Jocelyn's love for Thomas, laid bare in these letters, only fueled her fury. Ava was no longer just mourning; she was driven by a consuming rage that demanded retribution.

Jocelyn and Thomas had shared a love that transcended class and comfort. They had planned to escape together, leaving behind the trappings of wealth and status for a life of their own. Now, those plans were obliterated. All because of Oliver.

He had torn apart the future of two people in a single night. Oliver wasn't just a misguided soul; he was a psychopath. Hazel's warnings had been painfully accurate.

Before Ava could leave the library to warn the others, she needed a weapon. Her gaze locked onto Jocelyn's heart, the symbol of the love that had been so cruelly severed. She gripped the handle of the knife, her other hand holding the heart. She forced herself to ignore the sickening squelch of the knife sliding free and the blood that stained her skin.

Ava's eyes fell on the discarded leather sheath, and she snatched it up. The floral dress she wore, with its side slits revealing her thighs and ending just above her knees, proved to be practical for tonight after all. She slipped the sheath onto the back of her thigh, hidden but easily accessible.

She cast one final, sorrowful glance at Jocelyn and gently closed her eyes. "I swear I'll avenge you," she whispered.

Shouting and a loud thump from upstairs stopped her in her tracks. Desperation surged through her. She dashed out of the library, abandoning all pretense of stealth. She had to reach the others, and fast.

When Ava got to the top landing, she paused to listen. The shouting came from a room to her left. She ran to the door and flung it open.

"Guys, I know who the—" Her words died in her throat as she took in the shocking sight.

Edith stood beside Brandon, who was poised over Luiz's lifeless body, holding a candlestick smeared with blood. Brandon's face was contorted in a fierce, unhinged expression. Luiz lay on the floor, motionless, with a pool of blood spreading around him.

24

Before the Wellington's suicide, the chandelier that hung from the center of the spacious, opulently decorated guest room had sparkled brilliantly. Light from the grand window on the far wall would stream in, sending a cascade of dazzling reflections across the lavish dresser, the intricately carved wardrobe, and the other luxurious furnishings. Now, the chandelier's crystal drops hung heavy with dust, its once brilliant sparkle reduced to a dim, mournful glimmer.

Blood stained the large, dusty bed, the once pristine linens now marred with dark, splotchy stains. The former elegant walls, adorned with intricate patterns and fine wallpaper, were peeling and tarnished. Grime clung to the window panes, obscuring any remaining glimpse of the outside world, while the furniture, once a testament to wealth and taste, now looked worn and neglected.

Ava's voice reverberated through the room. "What the hell did you do to Luiz?"

Edith, arms crossed and face unyielding, gave her a disinterested look. "We dealt with the killer, of course."

The flatness in her tone only fueled Ava's mounting frustration and despair. The situation was spiraling out of control, and Ava felt powerless to stop it.

Throwing her hands up in exasperation, Ava shouted, "Luiz wasn't the killer! It was Oliver." Edith's eyes widened in shock, her mouth falling open in disbelief, while Brandon's gaze remained distant, as if Ava had ceased to exist in his world.

"No. No. No," Edith began to tremble, her voice wavering. "That can't be true. We killed him. We buried him." Her denial was palpable, mingling with the growing terror that Ava saw in her eyes.

Ava's voice cracked with desperation. "It's true. I found Hazel's diary when I was searching through her nightstand. Oliver visited his parents two years ago, before they took their own lives. They ended their lives out of regret for the beast Oliver had become. He's the one behind the murders tonight."

Edith's complexion drained of color. She tugged at Brandon, but he remained unmoved, his eyes unseeing and faraway. A sense of urgency surged through her as she cried out, "Brandon, darling, we need to leave!"

When he failed to respond, Edith's gaze shot back to Ava, her fear palpable. "What's wrong with Brandon?"

Ava's breath hitched, her chest rising and falling rapidly as she struggled to steady her voice. "I don't know. It must be the malevolent force in this house."

Edith's reaction was a chaotic storm of disbelief and hysteria. Her once immaculate hair had come undone, wisps of it falling into her face as she erupted into laughter. Her eyes, wide and glittering with a manic sheen, were framed by tear-streaked cheeks.

She clutched her stomach, her elegant, manicured fingers curling into fists as her laughter echoed off the dusty walls. "So, not only do we have a psychopath hunting us," she chortled, her voice rising to a frantic pitch, "but now we're dealing with a demon controlling Brandon?" Her laughter was jagged and desperate.

Ava realized her hands were aching from her white-knuckled grip as she balled her fists tightly. "Haven't you heard the voices? Seen the shadows acting strangely?"

Edith, her breathing coming in sharp gasps, shook her head vigorously, her eyes wide and incredulous. "Of course not! There's no such thing as demons or evil forces. Just... just psychosis and fear." Her voice quavered, losing its earlier conviction, as she struggled to maintain her composure.

Ava could almost feel the oppressive weight of the house's dark influence, sensing that it was selectively targeting those it intended to manipulate. If she couldn't convince Edith of the true nature of their peril, their chances of survival would rapidly diminish. Her mind raced, trying to formulate a plan to break Brandon out of his trance and save them all.

But she never got the chance.

A thud from the next room jolted their attention. Brandon, his movements unnervingly stiff, began to advance toward the door behind Ava. She quickly stepped in his path, staring into his vacant, amber eyes.

"Brandon, you have to snap out of it," Ava pleaded. "You'll die if you go through that door."

His face remained stony, devoid of recognition. Without warning, a high-pitched ringing filled Ava's ears as Brandon's hand connected with her cheek. She was thrown to the floor, clutching her stinging face as she lay sprawled.

Brandon continued walking, his movements almost robotic. Ava struggled to her feet, her vision swimming with dizziness. Ava reached out to Edith, forcing herself to focus through the haze of pain.

"We need to go," she urged, her voice steadier than she felt. "Oliver will be here any second."

As if on cue, loud thumps echoed in the house and Ava knew that Brandon was dead. Edith grasped her hand and they dashed out of the room. When they stood on the landing, they heard a door further down the hall open.

A dark figure emerged, the nearest candles flickering and dimming as he approached. The shadows in the hallway thickened and coalesced behind him, a dark tide rolling ominously. Voices began to swirl frantically in Ava's mind, and the shadows twisted and writhed on the walls.

Ava tore her gaze away from the advancing figure and sprinted down the stairs, Edith stumbling after her. They reached the bottom, and Ava lunged for the door, wrenching at the handle, only to find it locked tight.

"Who was that?" Edith's voice cracked with fear.

Ava snapped, "I already told you—it's Oliver! Why can't you understand that?"

Edith's face crumpled in anguish as she buried her face in her hands. Through her sobs, she managed to choke out, "I don't want to die."

Footsteps echoed on the stairs. Ava beat on the door with desperate, frenzied blows, her voice hoarse from screaming for help until her throat felt like it was on fire.

She turned toward the stairs, her heart pounding as the footsteps halted on the first landing. The thick, heavy shadows cloaked the top of the stairs, swallowing the faint glow of the candles and obscuring whatever lurked in the darkness.

A smooth, unsettling voice cut through the silence, dripping with pleasure. "Well, hello. Long time no see, Aunt Edith and Ava."

25

He continued, "I see you still have things on your mind, Ava. So, before I come down to kill you both, I'll give you a chance to say what you need to Edith." He let the words hang in the air. "But you'll have until I reach the bottom of the stairs."

Sweat broke out on Ava's forehead, and his threat felt like a physical blow. The certainty in his voice told her he wasn't bluffing. She turned to Edith, her eyes blazing with fury. "This is all your fault. If you hadn't drugged me, none of this would be happening."

A single footstep echoed from the top of the stairs.

She raged, "Because of your selfish ambition, I'm never going to see Carter again." Tears streamed down her face, and her body shook with ragged sobs. Ava knew that running and hiding would be futile. Oliver would always find them.

Another footstep echoed from the stairs.

Edith swayed like a leaf in a gale, her voice breaking as she wailed, "I refuse to believe Oliver is still alive. This has to be a nightmare. It can't be real."

Another footstep reverberated through the foyer.

And another.

Ava's eyes blazed. "You deserve to die. You're selfish, conniving, egotistical, vain, and pompous. Because of you, people died tonight."

Another footstep.

Another.

Another.

Ava thought of Duncan—forced into a deadly plot against his will, only to be murdered. The injustice of it all was suffocating.

Another footstep.

She thought of Carter—how he had lifted her up when she needed him the most. The future they might have had together, now forever out of reach.

Another footstep.

Lastly, Ava thought of Jocelyn. Killed simply for loving someone. Innocent and full of promise, her life was cut short by Oliver's twisted sense of ownership. The fire in Ava's chest roared into an inferno of fury.

Oliver descended the final step and emerged from the engulfing darkness. Ava's breath caught in her throat as a jolt of recognition slammed into her. She recalled her anniversary dinner with Carter, the unsettling realization that she wasn't losing her mind. She had indeed seen

Oliver across the street that day. The memory was sharp and clear: the same angular face, the same long, curly brown hair cascading to his almond-shaped eyes. His full lips rested beneath a short, round nose.

He wore a disheveled black suit, its fabric stained and worn. His white dress shirt was smeared with blood, a grotesque testament to the violence he'd inflicted tonight. Once-polished shoes were now caked in the grimy residue of countless deaths. Despite his casual, almost indifferent demeanor, his aquamarine eyes burned with a savage, feral gleam.

Oliver's mouth curled into a wide, predatory grin. His voice drifted through the room. "I trust you've had your chance to unload everything you needed to," he drawled. With a casual shrug of his narrow shoulders, he added, "It's best not to die with words left unsaid or regrets haunting you."

Edith's mouth moved silently for a moment before she rasped out, "B-but how? I killed you. You should be dead!"

Oliver's wiry frame shook with suppressed laughter. He chuckled, the sound cold and mocking. "Oh, you poor, naive fool. I was never dead. You only managed to knock me out. Had Brandon's blow been a fraction harder, perhaps then I would have died." He took a few deliberate steps closer, his eyes gleaming with a fanatical fervor. "I've been waiting for this moment for so long, dreaming of my revenge." His voice grew almost salivatory with anticipation, relishing the thought of their deaths.

Oliver drew a sleek pistol from his coat and leveled it at Edith's forehead. Her eyes wide, she began to plead for mercy. Ignoring her frantic cries, Oliver drawled, "Just as you had your brute of a boyfriend do your dirty work for you, I don't plan on killing you with my bare hands."

Before Edith could utter another desperate plea, Oliver squeezed the trigger. Her head snapped back and blood sprayed onto Ava's face. She jumped as Edith's limp body crumpled to the floor.

Oliver leveled the gun at Ava's forehead, a cruel smile stretching across his face.

26

Oliver's chuckles turned into full-blown laughter as he lowered the gun. He wiped his hand across his face, as if trying to clear away the mirth. The gun clattered to the cracked hardwood floor, its thud echoing in the foyer. He grinned, "Don't worry, Ava. I never intended to shoot you."

Ava took a cautious step back. "Why am I here? What did I do to deserve this?" She took another step, her back hitting the door. "What's the evil presence in this house? What happened to you when you vanished?"

Oliver, standing casually at the foot of the stairs with his hands in his pockets, clicked his tongue in mock disappointment. "Now, now, Ava. Why the hurry? We've got so much to catch up on." He sighed, his gaze growing contemplative. "But fine, I suppose I owe you some answers before I end your life."

Oliver's gaze locked onto Ava with a hungry gleam. "After my treacherous aunt buried me alive," he began, his voice dripping with venom, "I clawed my way out of that grave. I knew returning to the house would only put me back in her path, and at fifteen, who would believe me over my powerful aunt?" He sneered, a flash of contempt in his eyes. "Not that my parents would have cared, either."

He shrugged nonchalantly. "So, I set out, not knowing where I was going, and ended up in an orphanage." He took a step closer. "And as for the secrets—well, let's just say the house played a pivotal role in revealing them."

Ava breathed, "What do you mean?"

Oliver's lips curled into a sinister smile. "Oh, Ava, there's so much you don't know about this house. It revealed everything I needed."

Panic edged her tone as she asked, "But what's in this house?"

His grin widened. "I'm not going to tell you. In fact, I think I've said enough." As Ava's hand flew to the door handle behind her, she desperately hoped it might be unlocked.

"Wait," she stammered, "how did you manage all this alone?"

Oliver's eyes glittered with cruel delight. "Ah, this is my favorite part. I didn't do it all by myself. I met my partner in the orphanage where I ended up. You might know him as well." As he advanced, Ava twisted the doorknob. She nearly wept when it creaked open, only to be met by a solid, familiar presence just behind her.

The scent of cedar and musk reached her before she saw him. She turned and nearly collapsed with relief.

Carter's broad, muscular frame filled the doorway.

27

Relief washed over Ava at the sight of Carter's familiar face, but it was short-lived. A wave of sheer horror surged through her as Oliver's words sank in.

She staggered back, her voice breaking, "No, Carter. Please, don't tell me you're part of this."

Tears caked her face, and she fought to stay upright, her legs threatening to give way.

His grin widened into something dark and vicious. "Oh, it's true, Ava. I've spent the last year and a half dreaming of your end." The cruel admission felt like a knife twisting in her chest. "It was the only thing that kept me going while being in a dreadful relationship with you."

Ava choked out, "You don't mean that."

His face twisted into a serpentine mask of cruelty. "I hated every second of being with you."

The air felt like it was being squeezed from her lungs. She thought of all their shared moments, the small gestures that once seemed so meaningful.

Were they all lies? Did she truly mean nothing to him?

Her head spun with anguish, her heart ached with the weight of betrayal. She looked into the eyes that had once been filled with affection, now merely reflecting cold, unfeeling hatred. It was as though she was staring at a stranger.

She whimpered, "Why? Why are you doing this?"

Carter took a step closer, folding his hands behind his back. He sneered, "Well, partly because I relish in the act of killing, but also because you deserve this for abandoning Oliver."

Ava turned sideways, her numb brain trying to piece together the situation. Carter was the mastermind, and Oliver was merely a pawn in his control. Where Carter was unnervingly composed and in control, Oliver was consumed by barely contained bloodlust.

If she could exploit that, perhaps she could buy herself some time.

She fought to steady her breathing, forcing herself to stem the tears that flowed down her blood-stained cheeks. To gain more time, she had to appear calm, collected. She knew that this entire night was about terrorizing them. So, theoretically, the more unafraid she appeared, the longer she might stay alive.

Her gaze shifted between Carter and Oliver, searching for any sign of weakness she could use to her advantage.

With as much bravado as she could muster, Ava straightened her back and forced her tears to cease. She locked eyes with Carter, her gaze sharp and unyielding. "I didn't abandon Oliver. I was drugged." Turning to Oliver, she added, "I had no idea you were in danger."

A muscle in his jaw twitched, and annoyance flashed in his eyes.

His lips curled into a snarl. "You're lying! You knew how awful my family was. You were like family to me, and you didn't see the danger. You left me when I needed you the most."

Ava fought to keep her tone as disinterested as possible. "So, your answer to feeling abandoned was to go on a killing spree?" She clicked her tongue. "Ever considered therapy?" She hoped they couldn't hear the frantic pounding of her heart.

Ava turned to Carter, her voice ice-cold. "And you." She buried the sting of betrayal deep inside, her face a mask of defiance. "You use someone younger just to satisfy your twisted cravings for control? What's the matter, couldn't you do it yourself? Or are you one of those people who gets off on manipulating others? Well, congratulations, you've found the perfect puppet."

Carter's eyes narrowed, and his lips twisted into a tight frown.

Oliver interjected, his voice rising. "Hey! I'm not under anyone's control. We're partners, equals. I did all the dirty work tonight. I'm the o—"

"Shut up, Oliver!" Carter snapped, silencing him.

He turned back to Ava. "She's clearly stalling or trying to create discord between us. It's a desperate play. We should end this now."

Ava shrugged nonchalantly and drawled, "See what I mean, Oliver? You're just Carter's errand boy. You're under his thumb, and he's the one pulling the strings." She let her hands fall to her sides, making sure her fingers were close to the knife strapped inconspicuously on her thigh.

Oliver's face flushed a deep red, his eyes blazing with fury. "Shut up, Carter! I'll deal with her when I'm ready. Let's enjoy this moment."

Ava shifted her gaze to Carter. "So, whose brilliant idea was it to steal everyone's personal belongings? And the ironic deaths, really? That's kind of cliché, don't you think?"

Carter's narrow eyes, framed by a chiseled face and dark, tousled hair, narrowed with irritation. His jaw clenched as he considered her words. Ava knew she had to keep them off-balance and make them think she was less of a threat. She prayed they couldn't spot the leather strap barely peeking from under her dress.

He folded his massive arms and chuckled. "Those ideas were all his. He wanted to keep the belongings as trophies, or something like that. I thought they were pretty lame, but I let him have his way." The voice that once thrilled her now only sparked disgust.

Oliver stomped his foot, his face flushed with anger. "Shut up! They weren't lame. It was poetic justice. They got what they deserved. That was the whole point! If you don't stop insulting me, Carter, then I'll kill you after Ava. After all, I won't need you after this." His words were punctuated by spittle flying from his lips. Sweat beaded on his forehead, and his breath came out in ragged pants.

Ava glanced at Carter, her surprise evident, and scoffed, "Damn. Are you just going to let him get away with that? What kind of boss lets their underling talk to them like that?"

She hoped that a little seed of discord might sprout, maybe turning them against each other. But Carter's next words dashed that fragile hope.

He roared, "That's enough, Oliver!"

Oliver's face turned a furious shade of red. He clenched his teeth and his fists, muttering through gritted teeth, "Fine."

Ava forced herself to stay relaxed, trying to appear unshaken. With a dramatic sigh, she twirled a strand of her hair and taunted, "So, what's your grand plan? Drown me in the bathtub? Hang me from the ceiling? Stab me with a fire poker?"

Oliver's eyes gleamed with twisted delight as he spread his arms wide, clearly pleased by her response.

He smirked. "Well, since you fell asleep when I disappeared, I'm going to slowly choke you to death."

Seven Years Ago

28

Oliver gasped for breath as dirt choked his lungs. Terror shattered the fog of his disorientation, and he frantically clawed at the earth. It felt like an eternity before his hand finally broke through the surface. Exhaustion clawed at him, but he forced himself to keep going, fighting off the pull of sleep.

Air was slipping away.

Driven by adrenaline and raw determination, he heaved himself from his grave. As his head emerged, he coughed up clumps of dirt and mud, wiping his mouth with a grimy hand and inhaling deeply. The air was a revelation—sharp, cold, and invigorating.

He shook the dirt from his long, curly hair and surveyed his surroundings. He was in a moonlit clearing, shrouded in a dense fog that swirled around the bases of the dark, towering trees. The full moon cast an eerie glow over the desolate woods. He tried to piece together what had happened before his grim resurrection, but his ragged breaths caught in his throat, leaving him with only fragments of memory.

His aunt had tried to kill him.

A sharp, pulsing pain throbbed at the back of his head, and he winced as he touched his skull. His fingers came away smeared with dark, crimson blood. The sight increased his dizziness, and his mouth began to water. He jerked his head to the side, retching violently as the contents of his stomach spilled out.

Desperate thoughts began to take root. He needed to escape, but where could he go? Should he risk returning home, or would his aunt's murderous intentions still be waiting for him? What about Ava—had she been complicit in this betrayal? His mind was a whirlwind of unanswered questions, but he pushed them aside, focusing on survival.

A distant howl pierced the night

Oliver ignored the dizziness and nausea, forcing himself to dig out his legs from the dirt. Unsteady on his feet, he chose a random direction and started moving.

A cool breeze whispered through the silent, lifeless forest, sending a chill down his spine. The landscape was a bleak tapestry of gnarled, skeletal trees with twisted branches reaching out like bony fingers. The ground was uneven, strewn with fallen leaves and tangled undergrowth, and a thick mist clung to the underbrush, swirling with every step he took. The moonlight cast eerie shadows, elongating and distorting the trees into ghostly shapes.

Another howl pierced the night, closer this time, and Oliver's heartbeat quickened.

Anxiety pushed him to hasten his pace. The forest seemed to close in around him, the once faint rustling of leaves growing into ominous whispers.

After about an hour, he stopped abruptly, spinning in a tight circle. He could feel it—he was being watched.

A low growl rumbled nearby, and his spine went rigid. He didn't need to see the source to know what it was. The fog was thicker here, swirling around his ankles, and the shadows deepened, obscuring his vision.

Scanning the trees, he spotted a potential escape. One tree to his right, about nine meters away, had a low-hanging branch within reach. It seemed like his only option. If he could make it, it might just provide the height and cover he needed.

Oliver had one chance to escape, and he wasn't about to let it slip away. Today was not the day he would meet his end—not until he had his revenge.

He turned and sprinted into the depths of the dark forest. The mist clung to him as he raced forward, his vision locked onto the stark, gray tree ahead. He forced himself to ignore the snarls and growls reverberating through the trees, the chilling sounds of danger closing in on him.

With a final burst of adrenaline, Oliver launched himself toward the low-hanging branch. His fingers closed around it, and he swung up with all his strength, quickly scrambling to the branch above. He glanced down, his breath coming in ragged gasps.

Beneath him, five wolves stared up from the base of the tree. Their fur was a patchy gray, mottled with dirt and grime, blending seamlessly into the shadowy undergrowth. Their eyes glowed a piercing yellow, reflecting the dim light filtering through the dense canopy. Their breaths came in low, rhythmic growls, and their powerful muscles tensed with every movement, the faint rustling of the forest floor beneath them punctuating their predatory dance.

The wolves' sharp, white teeth were visible even in the low light, and their ears flicked back and forth, listening intently for any sign of movement. The soft pads of their feet barely made a sound as they circled the base of the tree.

Oliver's chest heaved with both relief and exhaustion. This was the second time he had narrowly escaped death—how many more chances would he get?

He edged back against the trunk of the tree, trying to steady his racing heart. The wolves below continued their vigil, and he knew he wouldn't be moving until they decided to leave.

Leaning back, he stared up at the cloudless night sky, the cold breeze brushing against his face. He wrestled with his memories, trying to piece together the events leading up to his awakening. He recalled seeing Ava asleep in the living room, her calm face illuminated by the sunlight that streamed in through the window.

His last clear memory was of his aunt, Edith, ushering him out of the house with promises of a trip to the city. But as they reached the bottom of the stairs, Brandon and Audrey, the maid, were already waiting.

Before Oliver could process what was happening, Brandon had struck him hard on the head with something heavy.

He had been slipping in and out of consciousness, knowing that any movement might mean they'd finish him off. At some point, he heard Duncan, the gardener, next to him, but Duncan didn't intervene. Oliver had no memory of what happened after they shoved him into the trunk of their car.

He glanced down to see the wolves still circling the base of the tree. Knowing he'd be stuck there for a while, Oliver made himself as comfortable as he could. He stared into the night sky, plotting his revenge.

❋ ❋ ❋ ❋ ❋ ❋ ❋ ❋ ❋ ❋ ❋ ❋ ❋

Oliver awoke to a gray, overcast sky. He half-hoped that the previous day's events had been a nightmare and that he wasn't actually stranded in the middle of nowhere, stuck in a tree.

But he was.

He rubbed his sore neck and tried to ignore the hunger gnawing at his stomach. Glancing down at the base of the tree, he saw that the wolves had apparently wandered off during the night.

Carefully, he climbed down to the ground, wiping his hands on his dirty brown trousers. The stench of dried blood and body odor assaulted his nose, making him suppress a gag. What he wouldn't do for a hot shower.

Oliver trudged onward, the gray skies and barren forest blurring into an endless monotony. As dusk began to settle, he finally stumbled onto a rain-slicked road. His white dress shirt, drenched in sweat, clung to him as the temperature dropped. Exhausted, he collapsed onto the damp pavement, gasping for breath.

Doubt slowly seeped into his mind. The thought of surviving another night in this desolate wasteland seemed increasingly bleak. Just as despair threatened to overwhelm him, he heard a rattling sound from the road's curve on his right. Blinding headlights pierced through the gloom as a car barreled toward him, showing no sign of slowing down.

Oliver hurled himself to the side of the road, but the car grazed his side before he could fully escape. A sharp, searing pain flared in his hip, and he let out a guttural scream. His mind raced—was it his aunt? Had they come to finish what they started?

Fury coursed through him, mingling with the pain. He refused to die here, not like this. He braced a hand against his injured side, wincing as pain shot up through his ribs. His hand came away slick with blood. He hesitated, then forced himself to inspect the wound.

A deep, angry gash ran from his hip up towards his ribcage, the blood flowing sluggishly. The wound was severe enough to be concerning, but the bleeding was relatively controlled. His heart pounded as the car screeched to a halt further down the road.

Oliver struggled to his knees, but his battered body betrayed him. Every movement sent fresh waves of agony through his injury. He looked around desperately, but the growing darkness and the dismal, rain-slicked road offered no solace. He was exposed, vulnerable, and utterly helpless.

Oliver's face contorted with indignation as the figure emerged from the car and stepped onto the road. A thick fog began to roll in, swallowing the night in its murky embrace. The only signs of her presence were the sharp click-clack of her heels against the wet pavement and the faint, eerie glow of her car's headlights.

His heart pounded furiously in his chest, each beat echoing his mounting helplessness as he waited for her to find him in his injured state.

After what felt like an eternity, the figure finally emerged from the fog. Oliver's eyes widened in disbelief. It was a nun.

He blinked rapidly, his mind struggling to process the sight of the older woman crouching before him.

She said softly, with a hint of panic threading her voice, "Are you alright? I'm so sorry for hitting you. I didn't see you until it was too late."

"I'm okay. Just a slight cut," Oliver chuckled, though the effort made him wince.

Her aged eyes, framed by thin lines of worry, narrowed as she tutted. "You don't seem fine. Let me see the wound." Oliver sighed but didn't resist. Her face turned pale as she examined the cut.

Oliver attempted a joke. "See? It's fine."

The nun shook her head with a gentle sigh. "Stay right here. I'll be right back." She stood and disappeared into the fog.

Minutes later, she reemerged with a first aid kit. Setting the bag down, she crouched beside him once more. As she opened the kit, Oliver took the chance to observe her closely.

She was dressed in a traditional black habit, the fabric dark and smooth against her pale skin. A simple wooden cross hung from a chain around her neck. Her head was covered by a matching black veil, and her face, though marked by the passage of years, held a calm and compassionate expression.

He guessed her to be in her fifties, her silver-streaked hair neatly tucked away beneath her head covering. Her fingers moved deftly as she pulled out gauze and a bottle of what he assumed was hydrogen peroxide, ready to tend to his wound.

She picked up the bottle of clear liquid and asked, "So, mind telling me your name and what you're doing out here by yourself?"

"My name is Oliv—" Pain flared in his side, and his vision swirled with spots. He gasped, "What the hell?"

She chuckled softly as she cleaned the blood around the wound. "I knew it would hurt, so I thought a little distraction might help."

He rolled his eyes, wincing as the sting intensified. "Yeah, because that definitely worked." Gritting his teeth, he took a deep breath and waited for the pain to subside. "My name is Oliver, and I ran away from home."

The woman carefully wrapped gauze around his wound and said, "I'm Claudia. I was on my way back to the orphanage I run." She examined her work, then stood up. "I assume you don't have anywhere to go, is that right?"

"No, I don't. I doubt my parents even know I'm missing," he replied, his face clouded with sadness.

Claudia scanned the desolate landscape, her weathered features showing a mix of resolve and concern. "Well, why don't you come with me? We have a nurse on staff who can take care of that gash properly."

Oliver looked around at his surroundings and quipped, "I don't have much of a choice, so why not?" Claudia chuckled softly and extended a wrinkled hand. She helped him to his feet, and together they walked back to the car in amiable silence.

Oliver glanced at the car that had hit him, a battered brown sedan. The vehicle's exterior was marred with scratches and rust, giving it a weathered, neglected appearance. Claudia noticed his cautious look and spoke with a hint of melancholy in her brittle voice, "We don't have much money, and this was all we could afford."

Oliver let her assume his wariness was simply about getting into a car with a stranger. In reality, his disdain was for the car itself—a far cry from the sleek, high-end vehicles he was accustomed to. The thought of riding in such an old, shabby car stoked his anger towards his aunt, who had stripped him of his privileged comforts.

The car door creaked open as he climbed in, revealing a stark contrast to the exterior. The interior was surprisingly clean and well-kept. The seats, upholstered in a soft, gray cloth, were immaculate and inviting. Despite the car's age, the cabin had a meticulous order to it, and a faint scent of lavender lingered in the air. Oliver sank into the plush seat, feeling the weight of his exhaustion. Drowsiness quickly overtook him, but he remained acutely aware of the blood seeping from his wound.

It was a miracle he was still alive.

Claudia's worried gaze flicked over to him as she said, "Don't you dare fall asleep, young man. I'll get us to the orphanage as quickly as I can. Luckily, we're not far, so hang tight."

She didn't wait for a reply before she revved the engine, popping a cassette into the radio. The car erupted with deafening rock music that blared directly into his ears as she slammed the gas pedal.

Oliver gripped the wooden paneling of the car door, the vehicle jolting into motion. He desperately wanted to drift off, but the stabbing pain in his side with every turn and the relentless noise kept him anchored to the present.

After a grueling ride, the car finally slowed, coming to a stop with a crunch of gravel beneath the tires. The music cut off abruptly. Claudia jumped out of the car and hurried around to his side. His eyes felt unbearably heavy.

She yanked open his door and unbuckled him with quick, urgent movements. "We're here, Oliver. Stay with me now, okay? Don't go to sleep." Her voice was a mix of command and concern as she shouted something toward the silhouette of the orphanage looming in the distance.

The haze in Oliver's mind thickened, making it hard to form coherent thoughts. Claudia gently helped him out of the seat, her voice soft yet urgent. "Keep pressure on the cut, alright?" He nodded weakly, though his vision was too blurred to fully make out their surroundings.

As she guided him towards the looming structure of the orphanage, her voice rang out in the night. Lights flickered on, revealing dark, shifting shapes rushing toward them. His legs grew numb, each step heavier than the last, but Claudia's grip remained steadfast. The approaching figures grew clearer against the foggy night, their hurried steps crunching on the gravel.

Oliver's vision dimmed further, a wave of dizziness threatening to pull him under. As the figures reached them, he felt the darkness close in, his strength finally giving way to unconsciousness.

✳ ✳ ✳ ✳ ✳ ✳ ✳ ✳ ✳ ✳ ✳ ✳ ✳

Oliver barely managed to crack his eyes open, a throbbing pain radiating from the back of his head and side. He winced and groaned, his vision swarming with dark spots. The room around him slowly came into focus—a small, square space with a homely but worn charm. The faded floral wallpaper was adorned with a few pastoral paintings, their colors muted by age. Scuffed wooden floors peeked out from beneath a ragged rug, while the modest bed he lay in rested on the worn fibers.

Claudia entered the room, her face lighting up with relief at the sight of his open eyes. She set a tray of food down on a plain white dresser beside the door, its surface cluttered with a few old knick-knacks. Rushing to his side, she asked with genuine concern, "You're finally awake! How are you feeling?"

"I need water," Oliver rasped, his throat feeling like sandpaper and his stomach a gnawing pit. Claudia quickly retrieved a glass from the tray she had brought into the room.

He sat up, drinking deeply and vowing never to take water for granted again. "How long have I been unconscious?"

"Almost two days," she sighed. "After you passed out, I thought you were dead. The nurse checked your pulse—it was barely perceptible. She stitched you up and bandaged your head. You've been in bed ever since."

Oliver mulled over her words, a simmering anger igniting in his chest toward his treacherous aunt, Brandon, Audrey, and Duncan.

And Ava.

If Ava hadn't fallen asleep, Edith wouldn't have had the chance to try and kill him. Ava was the only person he'd ever truly considered a friend—she was supposed to protect him from his awful family.

But she failed him.

He buried his hatred deep within himself, letting it fester and burn, ready to fuel his vengeance. Oliver forced a smile as he said, "Thank you for taking care of me. So, what kind of food did you bring me?"

Claudia brought over a wooden tray bearing a modest meal: a serving of beans, a few slices of roasted chicken, and a bowl of watery broth. Despite the rising disgust in his throat at the meager spread, Oliver ate every crumb. The food barely made a dent in his immense hunger, but at least he wouldn't starve to death.

She sighed. "I know you're still hungry, but that was all we could spare until dinner. Rest up, and I'll come get you then." Her eyes, though kind, were lined with the weariness of someone who had seen too much.

She carefully moved the tray from his lap to the simple wooden nightstand beside his bed.

As Claudia left, Oliver lay back down and let his thoughts swirl. The room, while clean and cared for, was different from the luxury he was used to. After she left, he lay back down and brooded over his predicament. To be in the care of peasants and not nestled in his large, plush bed

This was all Ava's fault.

Looking back, he wasn't surprised that his aunt or the servants had tried to kill him. After all, making their lives a living hell was his favorite pastime. What did surprise him was their actual courage to follow through with it. He didn't care much for the old maid or the stupid gardener, but he could begrudgingly respect their effort.

As sleep began to tug at him, he thought of the many ways he would exact his revenge, especially on Ava. The one person he had ever cared for had betrayed him to those monsters, and he promised himself she would suffer.

Just as he was about to slip into the sweet darkness, he felt a disquieting emptiness, like a piece of his soul had been ripped away. He hadn't noticed it before, but perhaps it was because he wasn't at home.

His house had always felt different, as though something else lived within its walls.

Before he could ponder further, sleep wrapped around him, pulling him into its velvety embrace.

✳ ✳ ✳ ✳ ✳ ✳ ✳ ✳ ✳ ✳ ✳ ✳ ✳ ✳

Oliver glared down at his plate of beans, rice, and roasted chicken, his lips curling in repulsion.

"What, you don't like the food?" A deep voice joked from across the table. An older boy with sleek, onyx hair, which framed his emerald eyes, plopped his tray down and settled into the wooden chair opposite him. The chatter of the other children around them was loud, making it difficult for Oliver to hear.

He hated the noise. The cacophony around him, combined with the throbbing pain of his still-healing wound, made his head ache. What he wouldn't give for some peace and quiet in this hellhole.

Oliver fixed him with a bored stare and drawled, "Oh, no. This is the best food I've ever had."

The other boy laughed and said, "I thought I'd like you. When I heard we had a new kid, I expected a sniveling little brat. But you're different." He pointed his fork at Oliver for emphasis and started on his bland chicken. "I have a pretty good read on people, and I think you and I are a lot alike."

Oliver raised an eyebrow, intrigued despite himself. "Oh, really? How's that?"

The older boy met his gaze with a knowing look. "I can see the hatred in your eyes, the desire to cause pain. I've got methods to help you channel that anger until you get out of here. Tell me, are you fond of animals?"

A tingle crawled up Oliver's spine at the implications in his words. The anger he'd buried inside was blazing uncontrollably, demanding an outlet.

He grinned wickedly. "Not particularly. But what if they notice we're missing or find...evidence of our activities?"

The other boy's grin widened. "Don't worry about that. I'll teach you how to blend in, how to fake being nice and kind. They'll never suspect a thing." He chuckled softly. "Speaking of which, I just realized I haven't asked for your name."

Oliver extended a hand across the small, worn table. "I'm Oliver Wellington."

He shook his hand with a firm grip and a smile. "Nice to meet you, Oliver. I'm Carter Bradshaw."

One And A Half Years Ago

29

Carter entered the bustling coffee shop, greeted by the comforting aroma of freshly brewed coffee and the gentle hum of conversations blending with the soft jazz playing in the background. The cozy interior was adorned with dimly lit Edison bulbs hanging from exposed wooden beams, casting warm pools of light on the mismatched vintage furniture and the chalkboard menu boasted a variety of artisanal brews.

Baristas clad in aprons moved gracefully behind the sleek espresso machines, their cheerful banter adding to the inviting ambiance. It was a haven where the rich scent of roasted beans mingled with the lively chatter of patrons, offering a sanctuary from the dreariness of the rainy, cold weather outside.

He scanned the packed, vibrant space for the bob of chocolate hair that would designate his intended prey. Carter had been following Ava for the past month, memorizing her schedule and frequent haunts.

She mostly spent her time with a tight-knit group of four friends, who seemed to occupy most of her social life. On days when she wasn't with them, her routine was predictably monotonous: work, then home. She was perhaps the most boring and depressed woman he had ever seen. He could already tell that he would despise her, though he rarely found anyone tolerable.

Carter finally spotted his target sitting alone at a small table beside a large window that nearly spanned the entire left side wall of the coffee shop. She wore a plain, white sweater with blue jeans and rain boots. To his satisfaction, he noticed her hunched over the steaming coffee cup in her slender hands with shaking shoulders.

He already knew the cause of the tears streaming down her distraught face. Oliver had recently told Carter about his visit to the manor to see his parents. Initially, Carter had been hesitant when Oliver presented the idea, but he allowed him to proceed. However, learning that his parents had died by suicide presented Carter with a perfect opportunity to insert himself into Ava's life.

He swept his long, black hair to the side and swaggered over to Ava's table, his brown trench coat flowing with each step. As he approached, he filtered out the background buzz of the café and focused solely on the woman in front of him.

He shoved his hands into the coat's pockets and said with feigned sincerity, "Excuse me, miss. Are you okay?" A thrill of excitement coursed through him at the thought of the long con about to unfold. It took a monumental effort to keep his face locked in a worried expression, one he had meticulously practiced for this moment.

Ava wiped her eyes and replied, "Yeah, I'm okay."

He chuckled softly to himself at her and remarked, "Right, because anyone crying alone in a coffee shop is obviously doing okay."

She rolled her eyes and said, "You know, if you're trying to help me feel better, you're not doing a great job." A smile tugged at the corner of her mouth. He grinned at the obvious banter. Maybe she wasn't as boring as he thought she was.

He smiled wide and joked, "I'd say I'm doing a pretty good job since you stopped crying." He paused and scanned her attractive features—the gentle curve of her lips, the delicate arch of her eyebrows. Her hazel eyes, flecked with golden tones, and her shoulder-length brown hair framed her face in soft waves, catching the light with every subtle movement.

A wicked idea crept into his mind.

Instead of being her friend, what if he became the perfect boyfriend that repaired her piece-by-piece?

Only to be reduced to rubble at the reveal of his betrayal. Carter fought to maintain the mask of a caring and concerned stranger at the vile thought.

Leaning in slightly, he asked with gentle sincerity, "Is it okay if I ask what's got you so upset? I'm Carter, by the way." He flashed her a soft, reassuring smile and extended his hand over the table. This was the crucial moment, the one where his performance needed to convince her of his genuine concern.

After a taut silence, Ava reached out and took his hand. "I'm Ava. It's nice to meet you. You can sit down, if you'd like." Carter let out a quiet sigh of relief, his ruse effective, and slid into the chair across from her.

And from there, the rest was history.

Present Day

30

Ava's stomach tossed and turned, but she forced her face to stay neutral. Carter stepped up behind her, his grip firm on both her arms. She battled the rising panic threatening to take over her chest.

With a bored drawl, she addressed Oliver, "So, you need Carter to hold me? Afraid I might put up a fight?"

Oliver's anger was palpable; his face was contorted, and his jaw clenched. He spat, "Let her go, Carter. It's not like she can escape. The house will make sure of that."

Carter's expression hardened, his body tensing behind her. His finger tapped thoughtfully against her shoulder. Finally, he released her arms with a huff. "Fine, do what you want."

Ava fought the urge to collapse in relief. Her gamble had worked, and with her arms free, a plan began to take shape in her mind. She had to sell it convincingly.

Carter turned and walked to the door, sliding the lock into place. He leaned against it with a self-satisfied smirk, the picture of arrogance.

Ava knew this couldn't be going any better, but she needed more distance between herself and Carter.

She cracked open the lid of the chest that held all the grief and trauma from the night, letting the weight of it seep into her voice. Tears streamed down her cheeks as she took a few deliberate steps toward Oliver.

"You're right," she said, her voice breaking. "This is all my fault. If I hadn't fallen asleep, Edith wouldn't have had the chance to try and kill you." She clutched her face, sobbing. "I'm so sorry, Oliver. Please, forgive me."

As she reached his small frame, she lowered her hands to meet his piercing gaze. Her fingers twitched with the urge to grasp the knife, but she held herself in check.

Not yet.

Oliver placed his hands on her shoulders, his voice low and almost tender. "I've waited a long time to hear those words, Ava. Thank you."

Her skin crawled at the wrongness emanating from him. Every instinct screamed at her to flee, but she stood still. The shadows around them seemed to pulse with predatory anticipation, blocking any escape.

Ava steeled herself, determined not to let fear show in her eyes.

She had promised Jocelyn that she would avenge her.

Oliver's hand moved with deliberate slowness, tracing the curve of her face with unsettling tenderness while his other hand crept toward her neck. His eyes, typically a deep russet, seemed to turn an inky black in the dim light, burning with a sinister satisfaction. He reveled in his perceived triumph.

Her fingers twitched at her sides, but she held herself back.

Not yet.

His touch became more intimate, as if she were a mere plaything to him, before his hand settled on her slender, sun-kissed neck. Ava could almost feel the chill of his gaze as his eyes promised nothing but a slow, torturous end.

Not yet.

As his grip tightened, his lips twisted into a grotesque, wicked grin. The candles in the foyer flickered, casting erratic shadows that writhed like a storm-tossed sea.

Not. Yet.

Ava only had one chance and she waited until she felt like she had no more air in her lungs.

Now!

With speed that only pure adrenaline and a strong desire to survive could provide, Ava grasped the knife her fingers had hovered over, yanked it from its sheath, and thrust it into his ribs with all the force she could muster, twisting until she heard a satisfying crunch.

While Oliver had been so focused on her face, he never noticed her hand drifting ever so slowly to the concealed weapon.

Surprise flickered across his face and the pressure around her throat lessened enough to draw a small breath.

Ava whispered, "That's for Jocelyn."

31

Oliver stumbled back, his eyes wide with shock and fury, but his grip on her neck remained unyielding. Blood gushed from his wound, spilling over her hands, which stayed rigid despite her trembling. Ava had hoped the shadows would recede once Oliver was wounded or dead, but instead, they thrashed violently, making the house feel as though it might start to shake.

She had a nauseating sense that the shadows—or whatever malevolent force controlled them—were like spectators, frothing at the mouth in anticipation, eagerly watching the chaos unfold.

She twisted the knife back and forth, desperate to turn his insides into mince meat, but his gaze remained locked on hers. Ava couldn't afford for this to drag on, not with Carter just steps behind her.

This had to end. Quickly.

After a few agonizing moments, Oliver's face drained of color, and his grip on her neck loosened. The stale air rushed into Ava's lungs, almost sending her collapsing to the floor.

She let go of the bloodied knife as Oliver fell to his knees, blood trickling from his slack lips. From behind, Carter's voice erupted in panic. "Oliver! What happened?"

It was now or never. Ava had only seconds before Carter's shock wore off.

Ava took a deep breath and bolted for the stairs, her heart pounding like a war drum in her ears. The swirling black shadows seemed to coil and twist, as if daring her to push past them.

She was nearly at the first step when she stumbled over an uneven floorboard.

32

The impact stole her breath, but Ava fought to lift her head and glare at Carter. He loomed over Oliver's still form, his white dress shirt drenched in blood. Malice and contempt gleamed in his green eyes, his jaw clenched tight and his mouth contorted into a vicious snarl.

Carter seethed, his shoulders bunched with constrained wrath. "I'll kill you so slowly you'll wish that Oliver killed you." He stood up and slowly stalked towards her, but Ava made no attempt to escape. "I'll flay you alive and carve out bits and pieces of you until there's nothing left." Spittle flew from his chapped lips, his features.

He was only six steps away when Ava's lips curved into a smirk. "I wouldn't be so sure about that, Carter."

Everything had fallen perfectly into place. She had lured him right where she wanted him, making him believe she was defenseless. That's why he hadn't noticed the gun she had deliberately fallen on top of.

"Oh, yeah? And why not?" he sneered.

Ava rolled onto her back and inched toward the first step of the stairs, the gun aimed at his chest. Carter froze, his brows lifting in surprise before he laughed. "You really think you've got what it takes to kill me?" he sniggered.

Ava stiffened and whispered, "Just answer me one question. Was anything we had real? Did you care about me at all or was I just a pawn to you?"

Carter's grin widened. "I despised you. I hated you. I fantasized about every possible way to kill you." His expression twisted into something grotesque. "I was just waiting for the day when I could drop the act and watch the life drain from your eyes."

Tears slid down Ava's face as Carter charged for her.

Her ears hollowed out, and something deep within her cracked as she pulled the trigger.

Carter's mouth opened in shock, and his hands cradled the wound in his chest as he stumbled back. Crimson blood leaked between his clenched fingers, and his mouth worked to form words. His knees buckled, and he sank to the floor.

He rasped, "This wasn't how this was supposed to go. We were supposed to win." His breathing started to hitch and slow. "It promised..." Carter fell onto his back and stared, with glassy eyes, at Ava. The shadows that surrounded them calmed and then retreated into the house, leaving Ava alone with the two dead bodies.

She looked at Oliver, his chest still and lifeless, and felt a wave of despair crash over her. Ava fell to her knees, staring at her blood-coated hands. Through her tears, she tried to scrub away the gore, but the crimson stains seemed impossible to erase.

She had killed them.

The realization hit her like a punch to the gut. She had ended two lives without hesitation. She had promised to avenge Jocelyn, but did that justify her to be their executioner? Was she now as tainted as Oliver and Carter? Was she still the naive, foolish girl who had walked in just hours before?

Her soul felt dark and oily, tainted by the weight of what she had done.

On her knees, Ava let out the storm of frustration, despair, anger, and betrayal that had built up inside her. Time seemed to stretch and blur as her body was wracked with sobs. When the tears finally subsided, she felt hollow, as if her soul had been drained.

She rose to her feet, moving mindlessly toward the kitchen. The gray, bloated figure of Cedric in the dining room and the horror-stricken gaze of Audrey in the kitchen went unnoticed. Why, despite everyone else being dead, did Ava feel like a ghost drifting through the house?

At the blood-splattered sink, she turned on the scalding water, welcoming the pain as if it might somehow cleanse the stain on her soul. When she was done, she turned and headed back toward the foyer.

She knew the butlers were probably waiting outside, but she didn't care. The thought of death was almost comforting—a release from the crushing guilt and anguish that bore down on her.

Ava opened the door and stepped out onto the front landing, surveying the decrepit landscape. To her surprise, there were no butlers in sight, and the sky was beginning to lighten. Perhaps they had fled after hearing the gunshot that killed Carter. Ava was too exhausted to consider the possibilities.

The dry, rancid stench of decay drifted on the chilly breeze. Ava sighed deeply and began her descent down the stairs, heading toward the nearest neighbor to call the police. Inside the house, the candles flickered weakly, casting eerie, dancing shadows on the walls, as though they were mocking her in their dim, flickering light.

33

The sound of Ava's heels on the road wasn't the only sound in the early morning. Unlike the Wellington's home and its bleak, lifeless surroundings, she now found herself immersed in vibrant greenery and lush forests. The contrast was striking. The lively sounds of nature—squirrels darting through the underbrush, birds singing their melodies, and the hum of other wildlife—brought the forest to life.

Ava had been walking for hours, each step heavy with fatigue, hoping to stumble upon a house. It had been so long since she'd ventured into this area that she wasn't sure which direction the nearest neighbor might be. Her feet ached, and she finally stopped to slide off her blood-soaked heels. The asphalt, damp from the morning dew, was cool beneath her feet. She closed her eyes, letting the warm sun filter through the canopy of trees that surrounded her.

Taking a deep breath, Ava pushed on down the desolate road. After some time, she came across a driveway tucked away in the overgrown brush. The entrance was unassuming, marked by two small brick walls that angled towards the continuation of the drive. Creeping vines clung to the weathered bricks, and small shoots of greenery poked through the gravel.

Ava hesitated, weighing whether to push on down the road or to check the secluded driveway. She doubted she'd find anyone living in such a remote spot, but continuing on in her current state seemed nearly impossible. With a weary sigh, she slipped back into her heels and carefully made her way down the driveway. The crunch of gravel beneath her feet echoed in the stillness of the forest

When she reached the end of the driveway, Ava gazed upon a quaint Victorian cottage that seemed straight out of a fairy tale. The charming home featured a steeply pitched roof with decorative gables, adding a whimsical touch to its appearance. Its weathered brick facade was adorned with intricate woodwork, including delicate scrollwork around the eaves and ornate trim framing the windows and door.

A cozy front porch, wrapped in a lattice of creeping ivy, invited visitors with its spindled wooden columns and an old-fashioned rocking chair perched invitingly. The multi-paned windows, framed by charming shutters, reflected the soft light filtering through the surrounding trees. A small, circular turret with a conical roof peeked out from one corner, enhancing the cottage's storybook quality.

The garden around the cottage was meticulously cared for, with vibrant flower beds overflowing with colorful blooms and a neat path of cobblestones leading to the front door. Climbing roses and ivy draped elegantly over the brickwork, adding a vibrant, green touch to the picturesque setting.

The beauty and perfection of the house stole Ava's breath away. She glanced down at her dress, caked with dried blood, and felt a pang of hesitation. The sight of the grime-streaked fabric made her doubt whether she could bear to enter such a pristine and innocent home.

Pushing those thoughts aside, Ava climbed the wooden stairs leading to the front door. She raised her hand to knock but hesitated. Why was her heart pounding so fiercely? After everything she had been through, why did this moment terrify her? What if the people living here were somehow connected to Oliver and Carter? What if this was another setup?

Lost in her thoughts and mounting distress, she didn't hear the door creak open.

An aged voice said, "Hello? Are you okay, dear?" Ava looked up, realizing tears had been streaming down her face. She saw an older woman, perhaps in her mid to late sixties, with a round, wrinkled face and straight, silver hair, crinkling in concern.

Ava cried, "I need help." Her shoulders trembled as the woman stepped outside and guided her in. The warm, caring touch released a deluge of emotion within her.

After she was guided to an intricately carved wooden chair at the dining room table, she noticed the chair's ornate design—its backrest adorned with delicate floral patterns and its legs elegantly turned. The rich, dark wood gleamed softly in the ambient light. The table itself was equally impressive, with a polished surface reflecting the intricate marquetry of vines and leaves that spiraled around its edges.

The old woman called out, "Harold, get in here!" Footsteps sounded to her left and paused, but Ava kept her head down.

A gentle yet firm voice broke through the haze. "Yes, Martha?" He paused, as if just noticing her. "Is everything alright here?"

"I don't know. This young woman was standing outside and said she needed help." Martha sat down and slid a steaming cup of tea in front of Ava. The earthy aroma and rich, malty notes of the deep amber liquid soothed Ava's frayed nerves.

The old man, Harold, settled into the chair across from Ava, concern etched into his square, seasoned face. He scratched his pudgy nose and asked, "Mind telling us where all that blood came from?"

Ava picked up the cup with quivering hands, taking a cautious sip. The warmth of the liquid slid down her throat and spread a comforting heat through her chilled body. She drained the cup in a matter of seconds.

"I was invited to a dinner party...and..." Her voice wavered, tears threatening to spill. She blinked rapidly, struggling to maintain control. "Everyone else was murdered. I was the only survivor."

Horror spread across her hosts' faces. Martha's hand flew to her mouth, her eyes wide with fear. Harold's bushy brows arched as he glanced nervously at the door, his sturdy frame tensing as if bracing for an intruder. He leaned forward. "What happened to the killer? Were you followed?"

"No," Ava breathed. "I killed them."

Relief washed over the couple. They exchanged a look of unspoken agreement. Martha, her voice steadier now, suggested, "I think it's best if we call the police. I'll get you another cup of tea while Harold handles that."

Ava thanked her as he stood and walked to the landline mounted on the wall. Martha set a fresh cup of tea in front of Ava, who sipped it gratefully while Harold's deep, gruff voice filled the room as he spoke with the officer on the other end.

After hanging up, Harold said, "The police will be here soon. Nothing to do but wait."

Ava nodded absently as Martha took the seat next to her. The older woman's presence was a small but welcome comfort to her troubled mind.

As the hour ticked by, Ava learned more about her hosts. Martha and Harold had once run this cottage as a charming bed-and-breakfast, which explained its pristine condition. The house was immaculate, from the spacious kitchen to the living room. The sink sparkled, kitchen utensils were meticulously organized, and the gray marble countertops were flawless. The tiled kitchen floor melded seamlessly into polished wooden planks that extended into the living area. Blankets were draped over the brown leather sofa with a deliberate neatness, and the whole space exuded an ordered, immaculate charm.

Ava also discovered that Martha and Harold had three children and nine grandchildren. Two of their children had ventured far from London, driven by a thirst for adventure. One now lived in Spain, while the other had settled in Germany. Their faces lit up with pride as they shared stories of their children and grandchildren, their voices tinged with warmth.

She was glad to hear that they were still visited regularly by their family throughout the year. Ava's heart ached with sadness at the unfairness of the family that Oliver had.

Her fingers idly traced the diamond ring on her hand, the once cherished symbol of their love now feeling more like a shackle. At what point would she find the strength to remove it? Could she ever bring herself to do so?

Despite the lies and deception from the very beginning, she had grown to love him. Ava's chest tightened as she grappled with the complex emotions churning inside her. She was uncertain if she could ever open her heart to anyone again, haunted by the shadows of trust that had been shattered.

Eventually, the blue lights from police cars bathed the kitchen in alternating flashes. A heavy knock echoed through the room, cutting off the conversation. Harold stood and walked to the door.

A police officer entered, his athletic build noticeable despite his short stature. He was accompanied by another officer, shorter and portly, with a stocky frame. The leaner officer scratched his scruffy cheek and said, "Hello, everyone. I'm Constable William, and this is Constable Peter." His eyes widened as they took in Ava's bloodied clothes. "We received a call about... a murder?"

Ava slowly rose from her chair, her feet throbbing from hours of walking in her heels. "Hello, officers. Thank you for coming."

Peter, the burly officer with a bulldog-like demeanor, cleared his throat. "Of course. Now, could you tell us the location of the murder?"

"The Wellington's manor," Ava replied. Shock spread across their faces, their mouths slightly agape, eyes wide with disbelief. Constable William's expression turned troubled. "No one's lived there in two years! What were you doing there?"

"Oliver Wellington never died. He survived the disappearance seven years ago and ended up in an orphanage. There, he met his accomplice, Carter Bradshaw, who was my..." Her voice faltered, but she forced herself to continue. "Fiance. Together, they planned a dinner party to kill everyone they believed was involved in Oliver's attempted murder. We were all forced to attend. I'm the only one who got out."

The kitchen fell silent, broken only by Constable William's raucous laughter. His partner, Constable Peter, shook his head with a weary sigh. "This has to be a joke," William said between chuckles. "It sounds ridiculous."

Ava's anger flared, her blood boiling. "It's true! The past twenty-four hours have been a nightmare," she snapped, her voice breaking as a wave of emptiness washed over her. "I've witnessed horrors no one should ever see."

Constable Peter ran a hand over his clean-shaven chin and exhaled heavily. His voice was rough like gravel. "Regardless of whether we believe your story, you're covered in blood and..." He gestured toward her with a meaty hand. "Something definitely happened at that house. Why don't you come with us?"

Ava nodded and turned to Martha and Harold. "Thank you for your hospitality."

Martha's blue eyes softened. "You're welcome, dear. I'm so sorry for everything you've been through."

Harold added, "Stay safe out there. You're welcome back here anytime." Ava's eyes stung with gratitude. She stepped out with the two police officers and climbed into their sleek, chrome-trimmed car, which gleamed in the evening sun.

Minutes later, as she settled into the plush leather seat, Ava noticed they were heading toward the Wellington manor. A chill ran through her veins. "Excuse me," she said, "but why are we going back to the Wellington manor instead of the police station?"

Constable William kept his eyes on the road. "We need to ask you some questions and gather information if your story checks out. Being back at the scene might help you recall details you could miss elsewhere."

Nervousness twisted in Ava's stomach at the thought of returning to that cursed house. She didn't want to go back. Couldn't go back. Constable Peter turned around in his seat, trying to reassure her. "Don't worry. Before we left that cottage, we called it in, and the station's sending additional units and a forensics team."

His large, round eyes softened. "You're not in danger anymore. It's over."

Ava exhaled slowly and leaned back, letting her mind wander as they drove through the twilight-tinted, forested countryside. Approaching the manor, she saw blue flashing lights illuminating the dry, cracked fountain in the distance.

As they navigated the long, gravel driveway, Ava felt the same unsettling presence as before. A chill raced down her spine, stirred by the malevolence radiating from the house. It was as if the force could sense her, its thoughts and emotions brushing against her mind. It toyed with her like a cat with a helpless mouse, mocking her with its sinister amusement.

Ava felt the force probing her mind, deliberating its next move. She remembered Brandon's vacant eyes over Luiz's body and was struck by a sickening thought: whatever was intruding on her mind could seize control if it chose to. Without warning, the presence abruptly withdrew.

Ava barely had time to process what had just happened before they came to a halt at the fountain. Constable Peter stepped out of the car and opened her door, letting in the dead, stale air that filled her nostrils.

"Let's take a look around while I ask you some questions, shall we?" Constable Peter's voice was brisk and matter-of-fact.

"Sure," Ava said, nodding.

She stepped out onto the gravel driveway, feeling the uneven surface beneath her feet. The manor loomed ahead, its boarded-up, decrepit facade bathed in the harsh light of the rising full moon. It looked like a beast waiting to swallow her whole.

As she walked toward the scratched, dusty front doors, Constable Peter and Constable William flanked her. Ava did her best to ignore the stares of the other officers on the scene.

"After everyone arrived, we were directed to the dining room by a butler named Charles," Ava began, her voice steady despite the tremor of fear beneath. Constable William scribbled furiously on a small notepad. "After we ate, about eight butlers snuck up behind us, guns pointed at our heads. Charles came out and threatened that if any of us tried to leave, the butlers outside would kill us." She ascended the stairs to the front porch and stood before the intricately carved wooden doors.

Constable Peter looked at her with a furrowed brow. "Why didn't you all try to band together to fight your way out or call the police?"

"The electricity wasn't working, which isn't surprising since no one has lived here in two years. And Oliver and Carter used everyone's secrets to ensure we stayed. If anyone left, their reputations would be ruined." Constable Peter nodded thoughtfully, his hand rubbing his rotund chin.

As Ava opened the door, Constable William asked, "Can you describe this butler, Charles?"

Ava's response faltered as she gazed into the dusty and grimy foyer. Her words died in her throat, replaced by a stunned silence.

It was completely empty.

There was no blood.

No Edith.

No Oliver.

No Carter.

Ava stood frozen, her eyes scanning the space where Oliver's body should have been. Panic gripped her, threatening to knock her to the floor. Could they have survived? The thought made her blood run cold, but she pushed it away. She had seen them die.

She turned to the officers, her eyes wide with disbelief. "I swear, their bodies were right here! Edith's, Oliver's, and Carter's were all in this room."

Before the constables could respond, Ava bolted to the left, heading towards the living room. She rounded the corner and sprinted to the dining room, expecting to find Cedric's body sprawled on the table amid half-eaten plates of food.

Instead, the massive table was spotless, no sign of a body, just dust and neglect. Her mind reeled as the officers' rapid footsteps grew closer behind her. Ignoring them, she dashed for the kitchen, hoping Audrey's body might still be there.

But the kitchen was empty. No blood. No body. There wasn't even an outline on the floor where Audrey's corpse should have been. Ava's heart raced with a sickening premonition that the rooms upstairs would be just as vacant.

The officers finally caught up, and Constable William, hands raised in a calming gesture, said, "Slow down, Ava. Let's talk this out."

Ava shouted, "They're all gone! It must have been the shadows or the butlers came back and removed all the evidence!"

Constable Peter raised a bushy eyebrow and huffed, "What do you mean by 'It must have been the shadows?'"

Tears slid down Ava's cheeks as she flung her arms out in desperation. "The shadows! The evil presence! There's something in this house that seemed to feed off what was happening here, and the shadows moved like they were alive."

Constable William muttered to Peter, "Go back to the car and radio the station. Tell them we'll be taking Ava to a doctor. I'll stay here with her." Constable Peter nodded and exited the kitchen, leaving her alone with William.

After a moment of tense silence, he began chuckling. His voice turned villainous as a slow smile spread across his angular face. "You know, I was quite impressed that you managed to kill Oliver and Carter. I wasn't sure if you were going to be able to."

Ava's mouth fell open, her voice barely a whisper. "Wait, you believe me?"

"Believe you? Darling, I was there. Who do you think was Charles?" He tilted his head, his sandy hair shifting with the motion, like a predator sizing up its prey.

Her stomach churned with fear at the menace in his eyes. "What do you mean? Charles was an old man…" Her voice trailed off as she scanned the room for an escape. The other exit was behind her, but she knew she wouldn't get far. If he was involved, how many of the officers outside were part of this?

William grinned. "I used makeup and a face mask to alter my appearance. I think I played the role rather nicely, don't you?"

Ava's mind raced. "Why? Why do any of this? What's the point? Who are you?" She needed to keep him talking until she figured out her next move.

He clicked his tongue, clearly pleased with himself. "I know how you managed to pit Oliver and Carter against each other. Impressive work, using their weaknesses to buy yourself time. I won't make the same mistake. Since you won't be a threat after we leave here, I suppose I can share a bit more. You see, I'm part of a special group with a unique interest in this house and its...resident. Oliver and Carter weren't members, but we used them to achieve our goal. It was crucial that you killed Oliver. We were taking a gamble, unsure if you could manage it. I say that because you were the only one capable of doing so."

Ava felt as if she'd been punched in the gut but steadied herself. Before she could respond, Constable Peter lumbered into the kitchen. "The call's been made. We can go ahead and take her."

Ava's fragile hope was crushed when William's gleeful sneer confirmed her worst fears. "Oh, did I forget to mention that my partner here is also a member of our group?" His round eyes sparkled with sadistic amusement.

Peter's laughter echoed through the room. "You finally told her? I loved the look on her face when she saw the foyer empty. I wasn't sure I could stay in character." He clutched his belly as he doubled over in mirth.

"No, no, no. This can't be happening." Her voice trembled as despair threatened to consume her.

Peter's voice was cold and final. "Oh, it's happening, sweetheart." He drew his gun and leveled it at her head. "Now, let's not make this any harder than it has to be. Just come with us."

Ava's legs felt like lead. The realization hit her with suffocating finality—there was no escape. Defeated, she crumpled to the floor as the two men approached, their faces lit with cruel delight. Silent tears streamed down her cheeks as they each seized one of her arms and hoisted her to her feet.

It was over.

But then she remembered Jocelyn and Duncan, the promise she had made to them. Anger flared in her chest as she thought of Carter's betrayal and the future that had been stolen from her. Her rage ignited into a blazing fire, fueled by the death and carnage she had endured over the past twenty-four hours.

With a shriek, she stomped on William's foot, causing him to shout in pain. He let go of her arm, and with it free, she swiped at Peter's face, her nails raking across his pudgy cheeks. Peter staggered back, clutching his bleeding face, and she seized the moment to run to the back of the kitchen, near the sink.

She grabbed a knife from the block next to the sink and turned around, only to find William blocking her path. His face contorted in anger as he said, "You really thought you could get away? There's no chance in hell you'll escape." Faster than she could react, his hand struck her face, sending her sprawling against the sink. The knife fell from her grasp and clattered to the floor.

William gripped her neck, pulling her back. She reached for the knife, but it was too far away. Dizziness overwhelmed her as she was dragged back toward the kitchen's entrance. Peter, with a towel pressed against his scratched face, glared at her with a smoldering, angry eye.

It was over.

William chuckled. "She got you pretty good there, partner."

Peter, his teeth clenched in irritation, snapped, "Shut up. Let's get her outside already." As they left the kitchen, Ava's dizziness began to subside, but William's grip on her neck remained relentless.

He leaned in and whispered, "Oh no, you aren't getting another chance. It's over, Ava." Her shoulders sagged in defeat as she was led to the front door. "The Cult of Belaroth thanks you, Ava." The name sent a shiver down her spine, a primal fear seizing her.

Turning to Peter, He asked, "Ready to put on a show?"

His partner grunted, "I guess. It won't be hard to act with the mark she left me."

William laughed. "That's the spirit." He pushed open the doors and announced to the crowd, "Sorry for dragging you all up here. It turns out this whole thing was just a prank by this woman." As they descended the stairs, the crowd's eyes were fixed on them. "The house is empty. When confronted, this woman attacked my partner." The crowd began to murmur as William continued, "She was ranting about evil shadows and dark powers in the house. Clearly, she's unhinged, so we're taking her to get some help."

Ava wanted to scream, to call for help, but she bit her tongue. Any outburst would only fuel the farce they were orchestrating for the crowd. The crunch of gravel beneath their feet was the only sound as they approached the car. William and Peter exchanged words with other officers, but Ava tuned them out, refusing to give them any more of her attention.

As they shoved her into the car, she cast one last glance at the mansion. Her heart sank when she saw a shadowy figure in the window of the second story, where the master bedroom was. The dim light of the night cloaked the figure in obscurity, but one thing was unmistakable: He was laughing at her.

34

Ava studied the doctor seated across the large oak table. He was middle-aged, with a clean-shaven face and shaggy brown hair that fell into an unruly mop. His square face, framed by thin eyebrows, gave him a distinctly angular look. The room mirrored his austere personality—modest in size, with a single window behind him, and a photo on his desk as the only hint of personal touch.

"So, why don't you tell me why the police brought you here this morning?" he drawled, his tone laced with boredom.

Ava's eyes flicked to the nameplate on his desk, noting that he was Dr. Robert Wilson. "I'm sure they've already filled you in."

He shrugged his broad shoulders. "They did, but I'd like to hear your side of it."

Ava struggled to keep her face neutral, weighing her words carefully. She knew she couldn't reveal the entire truth; doing so would ensure she'd never leave.

"My life was in danger. I witnessed people being murdered. The part about Oliver and Carter setting up a dinner party to kill their guests— that's all true," Ava said, her voice steady despite the unease coiling in her gut.

He raised an eyebrow. "And you're saying you killed them both?"

"I did."

"Then where are their bodies? Why was the house empty?"

Ava sighed. "I don't know. The only evidence I have is the blood on my dress."

Dr. Wilson leaned forward, intertwining his fingers. "The officers claimed the blood was from an animal. Are you suggesting they're lying?"

Ava hesitated, knowing that accusing the officers of lying could paint her as paranoid. Instead, she shifted the conversation. "Why not send my dress for testing?"

He leaned back in his plush leather chair. "I could have arranged for that, but your clothes have gone missing. Don't worry, I'm looking into it." Ava's eyes widened in surprise. She didn't believe that the missing clothing was due to a nurse's error.

He scratched absently at his beard, his gaze steady. "In the meantime, let me be honest with you, Ava. I genuinely believe something happened to you that may have caused a psychotic break. I don't think the blood you were covered in was from an animal, but I'm not entirely inclined to dismiss the police officers' account either. I suspect that what you experienced may have sparked delusions of a greater evil as a way for you to cope with the trauma. I want to help you, which is why you'll be staying here for the next seventy-two hours. Depending on how things go, we might release you or keep you for further rehabilitation."

He paused as a knock echoed through the room. An older nurse entered, her round, wrinkled face framed by shoulder-length, straight gray hair. Her eyes, sharp and assessing, flitted over Ava with a brief, almost imperceptible sneer. Was she part of the same cult that William and Peter belonged to?

"Hello, Dr. Wilson. I just wanted to let you know that Ava's room is ready," the nurse said, her voice as flat as her expression.

Dr. Robert waved a dismissive hand. "Thank you, Jennifer." Turning back to Ava, he said, "I think we've talked long enough. Please follow Nurse Jennifer to your room."

Ava's teeth clenched as she glanced at the nurse in the doorway. "Fine," she replied, her voice tight. She stood and walked toward the door with deliberate steps.

Jennifer's voice was curt but polite. "Just follow me."

Ava cast a final, pleading look at Dr. Robert, but he was engrossed in the papers on his desk. Sighing, she followed Jennifer down the stark, fluorescent-lit hallway. The lights were unforgiving, and a dull ache began to pulse between her eyes.

They navigated a maze of corridors and climbed a narrow stairwell, making several turns before stopping at a plain wooden door. A modest nameplate was the only indicator that this was her room. Jennifer opened the door and gestured for Ava to enter.

Ava stepped inside, her gaze sweeping over the bleak, utilitarian space. The room was sparsely furnished: a narrow cot, a metal chair, and a wooden desk, with a dresser tucked against one wall. The window was barred, casting a grim shadow over the small room. Ava's heart sank as she realized this was more of a prison than refuge.

Ava numbly sank onto the stiff, thin cot, her mind reeling from how her life had spiraled to this point. Jennifer's voice, cold and taunting from the doorway, cut through her thoughts. "Oh dear, don't look so sad. After all, you did a great service to our group." Ava's eyes snapped to the nurse, whose smile had twisted into something nefarious. "Don't worry, I'll make sure you're well taken care of during your stay here." Without another word, Jennifer stepped out, the lock clicking ominously behind her.

Fury surged through Ava, her body trembling as she fought to keep her anger in check. The realization hit her with a jolt: she'd been set up. William and Peter wouldn't let her slip away so easily—there had to be eyes on her. She shoved her rage into a mental box, reserving it for the moment she could turn it to her advantage. For now, she needed to maintain control, to bide her time until she could strike strategically.

Sitting on the cot, Ava focused on her breathing, determined not to let the oppressive confines of the room break her spirit. She would not surrender to despair.

She had a new purpose: to uncover the truth behind the Cult of Belaroth and the dark force that lingered in that forsaken manor.

Acknowledgements

First and foremost, I want to thank my incredible wife, Alexis. Your unwavering support and encouragement have been my lifeline throughout this journey. You've believed in me, lifted me up when I doubted myself, and pushed me to chase my dreams. I truly couldn't ask for a better partner.

I also want to give a huge shoutout to my beta readers, Dylan Bottoms, Madison Allred, and Samantha Edlund. Your feedback and insights were invaluable in shaping Twisted into what it is today. Dylan, your support has meant the world to me, and I appreciate everything you've done to help me grow as a writer.

A big thank you to Marcie Mabe for her amazing editing. Your keen eye and suggestions really brought my vision to life.

Lastly, I'm incredibly grateful to my parents for their unwavering love and support throughout my life and this writing journey. To my family and friends, your belief in me and encouragement have kept me going, and I appreciate each and every one of you.

Logan Hall

Logan Trent Hall is an indie author from North Carolina, soon to be relocating to London with his wife, Alexis, and their dog, Calvin. He graduated from Appalachian State University with a degree in Graphic Communication Management, but his passion for writing took off in April 2024. What started as a way to unwind turned into a love for crafting stories, especially in the thriller and fantasy genres.

When he's not writing, Logan enjoys spending time with his family and preparing for new adventures. He and Alexis are excited about their move to London, where they hope to use their skills to serve in the mission field. Logan is always thinking about his next story, eager to bring more of his ideas to life.